Slocum pushed east to find his scouts. Short-loping the roan horse, he pulled up at the flash of a mirror. Someone wanted him to know something. They were on the ridge to his right. He touched the gun on his hip, then sent the gelding off through the cactus and greasewood. Approaching the sheer face of a hundred-foot-high bluff, he wondered how to get up there.

No sign of his men. Strange they didn't appear. Then two shots rang out. The first bullet knocked him out of the saddle. Hit hard, lying on the ground, he saw the other bullets strike the dirt and gravel around him, sending up a cloud of dust.

A trap. Damn, where were his Apaches? He could only lie still and hope the bushwhackers rode on and did not check on him. In the distance, he heard men arguing in Spanish, but the words were too distant to make out. He knew only one thing—blood was pouring out of the wound in his side . . .

JAKE LOGAN

SLOCUM AND THE MESCAL SMUGGLERS

J

JOVE BOOKS, NEW YORK

THE BERKLEY PUBLISHING GROUP
Published by the Penguin Group
Penguin Group (USA) Inc.
375 Hudson Street, New York, New York 10014, USA
Penguin Group (Canada), 90 Eglinton Avenue East, Suite 700, Toronto, Ontario M4P 2Y3, Canada
(a division of Pearson Penguin Canada Inc.)
Penguin Books Ltd., 80 Strand, London WC2R 0RL, England
Penguin Group Ireland, 25 St. Stephen's Green, Dublin 2, Ireland (a division of Penguin Books Ltd.)
Penguin Group (Australia), 250 Camberwell Road, Camberwell, Victoria 3124, Australia
(a division of Pearson Australia Group Pty. Ltd.)
Penguin Books India Pvt. Ltd., 11 Community Centre, Panchsheel Park, New Delhi—110 017, India
Penguin Group (NZ), Cnr. Airborne and Rosedale Roads, Albany, Auckland 1310, New Zealand
(a division of Pearson New Zealand Ltd.)
Penguin Books (South Africa) (Pty.) Ltd., 24 Sturdee Avenue, Rosebank, Johannesburg 2196,
South Africa

Penguin Books Ltd., Registered Offices: 80 Strand, London WC2R 0RL, England

SLOCUM AND THE MESCAL SMUGGLERS

A Jove Book / published by arrangement with the author

PRINTING HISTORY
Jove edition / May 2006

Copyright © 2006 by The Berkley Publishing Group.

ISBN: 0-515-14129-1

JOVE®
Jove Books are published by The Berkley Publishing Group,
a division of Penguin Group (USA) Inc.,
375 Hudson Street, New York, New York 10014.
JOVE is a registered trademark of Penguin Group (USA) Inc.
The "J" design is a trademark belonging to Penguin Group (USA) Inc.

PRINTED IN THE UNITED STATES OF AMERICA

10 9 8 7 6 5 4 3 2 1

1

The roan horse dropped his head in the dirt to blow a puff of dust. Slocum read the sign on the storefront: GUNNER'S MERCANTILE. In the early morning coolness, save for the burro train peddlers selling firewood and water, the narrow winding street lined with stores stood empty. Above Bisbee's business district, located on the steep side of a canyon, jacals and huts clung to the slopes in the bushy junipers. Slocum stepped out of the saddle, wrapped the reins on the rack and walked through the open door.

Something was wrong. The notion struck him like a bolt of lightning. His hand went to the butt of his six-gun. Under his boot soles, the floor was strewn with flour and rice from torn sacks. Several airtight cans of tomatoes lay against the base of the counter where they must have spilled and then rolled away. Shelves had been stripped of goods in haste, for some items were strewn on the floor at the base of the rack. When Slocum peered over the counter, he spotted a dead man. On his back, arms outstretched, he lay in a pool of blood with his throat cut. Damn.

Slocum turned and headed for the door. On the street, he shouted at a peddler.

"Get the law. Someone's killed this man in here!"

"*Si*, senor." The man hurried down the street until he disappeared around the bend.

Curious women and men began to cautiously gather outside

1

the store. Slocum stayed at the hitch rack and smoked half of a small cigar.

"He dead, senor?" an older man asked softly.

"He's dead unless you can live with a slit throat." Slocum puffed on the cigar and tried to forget the ugly scene inside on the floor.

"He was a generous man—Senor Gunner."

Slocum nodded as a woman began to wail. "Who would kill such a fine man?"

"Thieves."

"Thieves?" She shook her head like that was unbelievable.

"Yes. They robbed his store, too."

A red-faced man in a suit was coming up the street led by the peddler. Though he looked to be in his forties and carried some extra weight around the middle, the man seemed tough enough to handle most situations.

"He in there?" The man paused and tried to recover from his lack of breath.

"Dead man in his fifties," Slocum said.

"You see anything else?" The man coughed into his fist.

"Someone obviously robbed him."

"The safe open?"

Slocum shook his head. "I never looked. Whoever did it stripped the shelves."

His hand on the door, the lawman seemed wary about going inside. "My name's Madden."

"Slocum." He gave the short butt a hard flip out into the street and moved to follow him inside.

"Jesus, they did rob the place," Madden said and walked carefully back to the counter, grains of rice crunching under his low-cut shoes. A sour look of disgust was on his face. "They cut off a couple of his fingers."

"I didn't see that," Slocum said from where he stood near the door. Death had no appeal to him. He'd already seen enough to last him a lifetime—especially the cruel kind in the store.

"Must have been torture to learn where his money was or to get him to open the safe."

"Yeah."

"Come in here." Madden looked up at him from behind the counter. He made a face at Slocum and waved his hands as if to stop something. "Tell them to stay the hell out of here."

Madden's threat stopped any invasion of the store by the curious. More rice grains crunched under Slocum's soles as he headed towards the lawman. When Madden made a face at something behind him, Slocum turned to see why.

"Jose, keep them the hell out of here!" The man scowled. "Damn, they'd loot the place if I let them in," Madden added under his breath and headed for the back room.

Slocum was on his heels. He adjusted the .44 in the holster on his hip.

"They went through here," Madden said, stepping over more abandoned items. Ahead, daylight shone from an open doorway leading out of the room to a narrow path between the back wall of the store and the rock face of the bluff. Madden looked up and down the alley. Then he savagely kicked a pile of fresh manure. "That's mule shit!"

"And?"

"That means some damn Mexican mescal smugglers did this. And they're boiling for the border."

"Madden? Madden? Where in the hell are you?" a voice came from the other room.

"Back here, Holden." The lawman made a scowl at Slocum. "He's the mine's security boss."

Another man in his forties wearing a suit came in the back room. Broad shoulders filled out the coat and his tie wasn't drawn up, as if he'd gotten dressed in haste. "They sure did in Gunner. Hello—"

He looked Slocum up and down.

"His name's Slocum. He found him dead about a half hour ago."

"Duke Holden."

Slocum nodded. The man never offered to shake his hand and he went out the back door to look around.

"Who did it?" Holden asked, coming back inside.

"Mescal smugglers," Madden said. "They wanted something to take back."

"The company will pay five hundred dollars for them dead

or alive." Holden looked back and he scowled at the mule manure that showed the thieves had been there for some time while
they tortured the man and loaded out his stock.

"Five hundred?" Madden shook his head in amazement.
"Guess the mine's got the deep pockets."

"We let them get away, it'll signal to any of them Mexican
banditos that they can come over here and get away with this."
Holden stopped and looked at Slocum. "Ain't that so?"

With a mild nod, Slocum agreed. "They'd probably consider it."

"Let's get a posse and a tracker after them," Holden said.
"The mine'll pay their expenses."

"They'll be in Mexico—" Madden waved the idea away like
it was flies.

"Hell with the borders. I want them brought back here and
hung."

Madden nodded. "You need work?" he asked Slocum.

Slocum shook his head. "Not to ride out of here with some
posse full of inexperienced men."

"You have a point."

"I'll get some of my guards from the mine." Holden
stepped in.

Slocum shot him a hard questioning look. "They ride horses
all the time?"

"No."

"Three days they'll fall out." Slocum shook his head at the
notion. He sure didn't need a passel of untried posse members
out in the desert.

"You know so much, where in the hell are some men you'd
take?"

Slocum turned to Madden. "You got any cowboys in the
jail?"

"Yeah, two, why?"

"Any ex-army scout Injuns hanging around?"

"Three or four of them around town. Why?"

"Round them up—" He stared at the sun to calculate the
time. "Outfit them. Get a couple of pack animals and enough
supplies for three weeks."

"What the hell're you suggesting?" Holden made a face like
he was suspicious of the deal.

"You want these killers brought in?" The man's attitude was grinding on Slocum's patience.

"I said so."

"Then send a force out there that will bring them in."

"What do you think?" Holden asked Madden.

"I don't know a thing about the man. This is the first time I laid eyes on him, but he makes sense to me. You and I sure as hell won't make it three days in the saddle out there."

"You got any credentials?"

"If I had would I be here?" Slocum smiled at him and slowly shook his head in disbelief the man would even ask for any.

"How do I know that you won't take it all and run?"

"You don't."

Holden shook his head as if to dismiss his words. "Where will you be?"

"I kind of figured you might put me up in the local cathouse while you cleared all this with your bosses." Slocum looked hard at the man.

Madden had to turn away to suppress his amusement.

Holden reached in his coat and drew out a card. He used a pencil to write on the back: *Give him what he wants—Holden.* "Here. Ruby's Place is down the street, one block on the left, upstairs."

Slocum nodded.

"I suppose you want them armed with repeating rifles?"

Slocum stopped in the doorway. "If you want us to capture or kill them."

"I'll have 'em at the city jail by five o'clock. You can pick who you want out of them. Five o'clock, hear me?"

Slocum nodded, untied the roan, mounted and started off down the steep, crooked street. He owned a few hours of his own and a free pass to pleasure. Better soak up all he could—there'd soon be enough hell to last him a long time.

"You better not double-cross me either!" Holden shouted after him.

The roan boarded at Slade's Livery, while Slocum bought a fresh-made bean and meat burrito from an older woman who was cooking in the street. He paid her ten cents and set off up the crooked, narrow street for Ruby's Place.

He stopped at the entrance and looked up the long flight of

enclosed steps. He'd bet she'd lost a few drunk customers on them. Wrong time of day for such an establishment, but what the hell, they'd get someone up—no need to piss off the powers that be. He rapped on the door at the top of the stairs.

"Who the hell's there?" someone shouted out.

"A customer."

"Gawdamnit, we're closed."

"Mr. Holden sent me."

"That no-good dumb sumbitch knows—" A woman in her thirties wearing a lacy blue nightgown jerked open the door, threw her head back and blinked at him.

He handed her the card and removed his hat. Inside, he could see the living room was empty.

"Who in the hell're you?" She looked him over from head to toe. "He usually sends city stiffs up here with a card like this. Mine Company bigwigs. You look like you just rode in out of the damn desert."

"I did about an hour ago."

She flicked the card at him and gave a know-it-all smile. "You're either damn important or you've got Holden over a barrel and he's saving his ass with both hands."

"Which way gets me the best lay?"

"Honey, all I've got are the best."

"Fine. Where is she?"

She turned, waved over her shoulder for him to follow her and started down a hallway. At the second door, she used a key and eased it open, peeked in, then shook her head. Door closed, she said, "That bitch is dead to the world."

Slocum nodded. Two more doors and she tried the knob, it opened. She stuck her head in and laughed. "Got you a hot one, baby."

"This is Lucille," she said stepping back and ushering him in the room. "She knows what it's for, mister. Never caught the name?"

"Slocum."

"Probably not with her." Ruby threw her head back and laughed aloud.

Lucille sat in the middle of the bed. Her bare legs crossed, she was finishing a game of solitaire on the sheet. She swept the honey brown hair back from her face and smiled. "We've never met before."

"Slocum," he said, admiring the pear-shaped breasts that were barely covered by the open front of her duster.

In one scoop, she rounded up all the cards and leaned over to put them on the nightstand, exposing her shapely bare legs. Then she unfolded off the bed and stepped toward him. "Well, Slocum, you didn't come up here to see me play cards, now did you?"

She took hold of his vest and gave it a jerk down. "You came up here for action." One hand covered a yawn, and she shook her head. "I mean real action."

He nodded as she ran her hand over the mound in his pants. Mischief danced in her violet eyes when she squeezed it.

"And this ain't your first time either." She swept her hair back and laughed. "No, siree. This ain't number one." She let him undo the gun belt and hang it on the bedpost, then she gave him a shove on the bed and began to fight his boots off. Standing astraddle his leg, she worked the right one off, then picked up the left one. With a hard twist, she freed his foot and dropped the boot with a clunk to the floor. Then she dove in and undid his belt. Buttons she tore open and grinned at him when he gently fondled her breasts that swung free.

"I'm impressed. Most men grab at them like they were apples to pick." Taking hold of the hem at the bottom of the legs, she hauled off his pants. Then came his vest and the collarless shirt she hung on the back of the wood chair. She snuggled up against him and began undoing his one-piece underwear a button at a time.

"Where do you hang that old weather-beaten hat of yours?" she asked.

"On any old bedpost I can find," he said, slipping the duster off her shoulders.

She drove a rock hard breast into him when she removed the top portion of his underwear. Then, bending over to strip the rest down, she breathed fire on his turgid dick. "Oh my gawd, this is going to be fun."

Slocum then stood and the cool morning breeze swept over his bare butt. He took Lucille in his arms and nuzzled up her neck. Her fist clasped tight around his pointed erection, she nibbled on his shoulder.

"Let's get in bed," she whispered, tracing her nail-hard nipples over his chest.

"Fine," he agreed, ready to stick his throbbing sword to her.

She dropped hard on the mattress, making the ropes squeak and then scooted backwards until her honey hair was fanned on the pillows. Snow white long legs spread apart, she gave him a welcome smile and held out her arms for him.

Slocum came to her on his knees and grinned back. He hovered over her and she guided his prod into her slick gates. He began to pump and soon both of them were deeply engrossed in the fury of their efforts. His butt ached to poke his sword clear through her; she arched her back and pressed her pubic bone against his for more. The bed ropes protested beneath them and their grunting grew louder. Faster, harder, more. Despite the cool temperature in the room, sweat began to grease their bellies. Suddenly, she clutched at him and cried out, "Yes, yes!"

His cannon fired. Hot fluid began to flow from her and the depths of his scrotum until it exploded out of his cock. It felt like molten lava spewing inside her tight pussy. They both collapsed in a pile.

He swept the hair back from her face and kissed her forehead, cheeks, than finally her mouth and she clung to him with all of her might. At last they lay in each others arms and napped.

He still had until five o'clock.

2

They were in the narrow alley behind the three-story court-house. Six Indians. Holden introduced each one.

"This is Dio," he indicated the short thickset one, who nod-ded holding his beat up straw hat in front of his chest.

"Apache?" Slocum asked, using the Indian word *dine.*

The man said, "*si*," and made a firm nod that he was satisfied at Slocum calling him that word for his people.

Holden waited until Slocum motioned for him to introduce the next one.

A boy of perhaps eighteen. Small and sinewy, he looked de-fiant as Slocum recalled the way Geronimo acted in Mexico when he met with General Crook. Hatless, the youth wore a loincloth and an old faded blue shirt with a silver cross strung around his neck on a rawhide thong.

"He calls himself Black Wolf."

"Can you shoot a rifle?" Slocum asked him in Apache.

"I can shoot a lizard's eye out at great distance."

Some of the others laughed. Holden obviously did not un-derstand the language and shrugged. "You want him?"

"I'll see." Slocum pointed to the third man and thought he saw someone he knew. "Joe?"

"You remember me from the mother mountains. I saved your life one time," the wrinkle-faced older man said in his own dialect.

"Above Saint Ann's Mission in Paco Canyon. They shot my horse out from under me and you came back and got me." Slocum nodded. "I can remember that day well."

Joe grinned big.

"You want to sleep on the ground and eat sand-gritty frijoles down there again?" Slocum asked.

"It pays, I go."

"Be—where will they get their horses?" Slocum, realizing the Indians were probably afoot, asked Holden.

"Livery."

"Be there before sunup," Slocum said.

The Apache smiled and agreed.

The next two were drunks and showed no real interest in going to Mexico in a posse. Number six squatted in his knee-high boots and never looked at Slocum. He wore a red kerchief for a headband and he acted as if his spirit were elsewhere.

"You have problems?" Slocum asked the one that Holden called Little Hawk.

"A *bruja* has taken my soul."

"What does this witch want?"

"Money and horses, she says."

"Will she still have a spell on you in Mexico?"

He shrugged.

"We leave in the morning. Do you wish to go?"

"I will listen for a sign."

"What did he say?" Holden asked, acting a little aggravated or bored by the whole thing of hiring Apaches.

"He needs a sign."

"Sign for what?" Holden made a disgusted look.

"He may or he may not show up," Slocum said to settle the matter.

"Damn, you can even talk that shit to them. Who else do you want?"

"Dio? You want to go?" Slocum asked.

"*Si*." The man's broad face lighted up.

"Good. You, Black Wolf, Joe, and Little Hawk, if he gets a sign."

"That enough?" Holden asked.

"Enough trackers. You got some cowboys?"

"Upstairs in the jail."

"See you in the morning," Slocum said to them. After they all nodded in agreement to be there, even the boy, Slocum followed the mine man.

"My people are anxious. They're on my ass asking why you ain't left yet." Holden gazed up a steep set of stairs they needed to climb.

"You get in hot pursuit, they'll scatter like a covey of quail and you won't get but a few of them. Let them think they've gotten away with it and they'll stay together."

"Yeah, that makes sense. Obviously you've been with Apaches."

"Crook in Mexico."

"Yeah, I figured that with you talking to them like that," Holden said over his shoulder as they hiked the steep steps.

They entered an office where two obvious cowboys were slumped down in chairs against the wall. One had a bad black eye and the other a bandage on his head. Early twenties, Slocum sized them—one short, the other tall.

"They tell you what he needs?" Holden asked the desk man who nodded and went back to his paperwork.

"You bail us out of here, we might even herd sheep," the short one said.

"What's your names?" Slocum asked.

"Roy Smears and this guy under the bandage is Sid Black."

"It's going to be tough going. They're headed for Mexico." Slocum waited for their reply.

"We don't care. We can ride and handle it."

"These smugglers aren't your run-of-the-mill barroom brawlers. They're killers."

"We savvy that, too," Roy said.

"What about you, Sid?" Slocum asked the bandaged one.

"I savvy enough to know it'll be hell."

"Good, you two be at the livery at four in the morning, ready to ride."

"I'll come bail you out before then," Holden said.

"Not now?" Roy asked, disappointed.

"Hell, no. I'll be here in plenty of time you won't miss the ride out of town."

Roy stuck his hand out and shook with Slocum; so did Sid.

"We sure appreciate it," the cowboy said and his partner agreed.

Holden spoke to the jailer and then nodded to Slocum. "That's taken care of. Let's go check on your supplies."

"Suits me," Slocum said and grinned at the man. No stranger to Mexico, he had his choice—cowboys and Indians. They could ride all day and not complain, wouldn't bitch about the grub and might even bring in the bad guys.

"Four blanket-ass Injuns and two worthless cowboys." Holden shook his head in disbelief as they walked the uneven stone-paved sidewalk. "You really think you'll find them killers?"

"I wouldn't even leave here if I didn't think we had better than a fifty-fifty chance of capturing them."

Holden stopped before the large mercantile store. "Why ain't we never met before?"

"Guess we ain't frequented the same places. This it?"

"Yeah, the company store. You got any idea what you need?"

Slocum nodded and pushed inside. "I know exactly what to order. You got four mules?"

"That's what you need? Not burros?"

"No, mules."

A young man who knew Mr. Holden waited on them. Slocum began to list his needs: flour, baking powder, brown sugar, rice, frijoles, bacon, airtight tomatoes and peaches, raisins, dried apples, coffee, canned milk, salt, pepper and red chili string.

"You got some cooking gear we can use?" Slocum asked the man

"Like?"

"Dutch oven, couple of cooking pots, coffeepot, wooden spoons and a few big knives?"

"I'll have them there."

"Horseshoe nails and a hammer," he said to the clerk on his way after something.

"Coming right up, sir."

"You know outfitting," Holden said. "You must have done this before."

"You want those killers brought in?"

"Hell, yes. I ain't wasted the damn evening being social with you."

"Then stop worrying who I am."

"Man in my boots got to know everything to cover his ass. They don't take almost or nearly for an answer up at that fucking mine office. They want results." He used his finger to point at his chest. "It's my ass that goes up in smoke if this fails, not yours."

"Well, you and the marshal and some good old boys could have ridden down there and come back coated in dust, too, with your tails between your legs. All you need to know is I'm going after them."

"No, I've got to account for every dime I spend here, the livery and even your toss in the hay with some whore."

"You should try her some time. She's lovely." Slocum nodded to the youth who'd returned with his goods. "Need some matches and two small cans of coal oil."

"Which one?" Holden asked when the clerk was gone.

"Lucille."

"I'll do that."

"I think that's everything," Slocum said when the boy returned. He turned to Holden. "Don't you forget the cooking stuff."

"I won't."

"See you at four in the morning." Slocum gave him a salute off his hat brim.

Holden shook his head in disgust. "I'll be there."

After supper in a cafe, Slocum took a hotel room for the night with orders to wake him at three A.M. The night proved short and he barely could open his eyes to the rapping on his door.

"Okay, okay," he said and it stopped.

No place to buy coffee since no cafe was open, so he was grateful for the livery man's offer of some that was a cross between tar and dead stump juice. Still, he sipped it and oversaw the packing by the two cowboys. The mules were stout mine animals and, while they had the usual disposition, they stood well despite their honking during the loading process in the cool predawn air.

"Cook gear here?" Slocum asked as they worked under coal oil lanterns.

"On the mare mule," Roy said; he had taken charge.

"Got enough?" Slocum asked.

"It's all there."

"Fine." Slocum stepped back as Sid brought more out to put away in the panniers.

"Worst damn coffee—" Holden shook his head and tossed the full cup in the street. "I counted three Injuns."

"Three will do. The other one may come later."

"What's his damn problem?"

"Some witch has a spell on him."

"Lazy ass for my money."

"Spells are real to all Indians."

"I don't believe in them."

"That's 'cause you never been under one." Slocum went to lead out the roan and saddle it.

"I'll find you when I have one on me," Holden said. "You sound like you know all about them."

"Do that," he said over his shoulder, headed for his horse.

"All bullshit!" Holden shouted over the mules braying.

Slocum hoped the man never found out how bad they could be. But sooner or later, living on the border like he did, someone he pissed off would hire a *bruja* to cast a spell on him. A powerful enough one would drive him mad unless he sought help.

The roan saddled, Slocum selected a rifle from the stock Holden brought. The lever action felt tight and smooth. It had been well cleaned and oiled. He slid it in the new scabbard and tied it under his right stirrup. Two boxes of fresh cartridges in his saddlebags and he went to arming his Apaches, who picked out horses to ride.

"If there's anything left when this is over, bring it back. I may get part of the money I spent refunded," Holden said.

Slocum nodded. It would be an hour before the sun tried to peek out on them. He wanted to be to the top of the pass by then. There he figured they'd cut down the spine and head south for Mexico.

"Joe," he said, gathering his Apaches, "we'll ride to the pass and get their trail. Meet me in camp on the Santa Cruz side of the border." He indicated to the three of them and they nodded. "Find their tracks. They had a train."

"Come get you when we find them?" Joe asked.

"Yeah." He didn't expect to be that close to them for a couple of days.

An hour later in the pass, a cooling wind swept his face. Five mules and the two cowboys were in good shape for the steep haul. He'd forgotten the damn braying the mules made all the time and the cussing they received for it from their handlers. Been awhile since he'd been involved with such an outfit.

Both cowboys had dismounted and were walking some kinks out of of their legs. Hands on their hips, their spell in jail must have stiffened them up.

"You see our tail?" Slocum asked, looking back down the deep canyon they'd emerged from.

"Hell, no, who is it?" Roy asked, heading to look down the back trail off the rim.

"I think it's a squaw."

"Long as she's only after my pecker and not my scalp, I'll take her," Roy said and chuckled.

"She may belong to one of them three up ahead."

"Hell, I was so busy skinning them mules I never noticed," Sid said, adjusting the crotch in his pants and chaps. "I'd better wake up."

"Won't be a bad idea. But anyway, if she was just coming over this mountain, she wouldn't stop and then disappear in the juniper brush whenever she gets close to us."

"What are you going to do about her?"

"She follows us down this spine, I'll drop back and rope her when she rides past me."

Roy hitched up his pants and looked over the mountaintop to the south. "I've never been this way."

Slocum nodded. "It's not wonderful, but you can make it. I been over it a dozen times chasing Apaches with the army."

"How far is that spring on the Santa Cruz?"

"Maybe ten miles." Slocum could see the Huachuca Mountains in the distance. The breeze felt good. He hated to leave it. "We better get these mules moving."

"Right," Roy said, taking the lead of the first mule. "You drive 'em, Sid, and we'll switch off down the trail."

"Go ahead. I may trap her and find out why she's following us," Slocum said, turning the roan aside. Whoever she was, he wanted to know.

3

He sat the hip-shot roan in the grove of stunted pine and junipers. The slap of the unshod horse on the rocks drew closer. He could hear her cussing it in Spanish, then the sound of a quirt being applied to make it trot. Without seeing Slocum, she rode past his hiding place on her slab-sided pony. Her bare heels beat his ribs like a drum. Slocum sent the roan charging out and snatched her bridle reins. Then he used his other hand to grasp the quirt and wrench it away from her. The fury in her coffee-colored face looked like a mountain lion unleashed.

"You! You bastard. Give me my reins and my whip back." Hands on her hips, she gave him a withering glare that would have melted a block of ice.

"Why are you following me?"

"I follow no one!"

"Lady, I been watching you for two hours, don't lie to me."

"This is a free country. I can go anywhere I want to go." She gave a shudder like she was getting rid of him with her reply. Brown arms folded over her fine-looking breasts, clad under a white cotton blouse, she gazed past him at the distant valley like he wasn't even there.

"I asked why you following me."

"They said you are going to Mexico."

"Hell, girl, there are easier routes than this way to Mexico."

"A free—"

"A free country, right. But when you come up my back trail, you need a reason."

"Who said I was going there?"

"Why are you tracking us?"

"Everyone in town said you were going after the smugglers."

"You want me or them?"

She gritted her teeth and looked ready to get enraged. "Those bastards killed my husband Enrico the last time they came up here. I was hoping this time they would stay long enough for me to plan an ambush for them."

"Why follow me?"

"If you are going to arrest them—" She shrugged and looked away. "I want to kill that murdering devil, El Maldito, and I would do anything to get the chance."

"I'll get him dead or alive, but you can't kill him if he's my prisoner."

"He's not worthy to live."

Slocum shook his head. "You can go along with the men. But you can't plan to kill him when he's my prisoner."

"Why would you let such a butcher live?"

"What is your name?"

"Mary. Mary Vasquez."

"Slocum. Now you heard my terms. I can pay you some money to cook. But I don't want anyone murdered in my custody."

She closed her eyes and nodded. "How long will this take?"

"A week or a month. We don't care, just so we get them."

"So you get them," she agreed and acted submissive enough that he believed her.

"Mary, let's ride for the camp." He handed her the reins and quirt, wondering if he would ever regret giving them back to her.

He turned the roan southward and they headed across the juniper-studded mountain skirting around gnarled live oak, sage and dry bunch grass. The trail was worn down from hundreds of years of Apache movement back and forth to their haunts in Mexico.

The Apaches had brought back captive women and children over this route. Slocum could see the prisoners struggling to walk fast enough behind the horses—all massed in a line with raeta tied around their necks, an Apache woman on horseback with a whip lashing any that looked like they would straggle.

The smart of the lash drove fainting from their muddled minds. Water must have occupied their every thought for their captors could go forever on little moisture.

Dust-floured and disheveled, some were half-naked from abuse. The virgins were all raped. Babies cried. Many had been held by the heels, their heads bashed like watermelons on rocks days before. Tiny corpses were left behind for the low flying buzzards that glided over the march and waited for another meal. Past hungry, the slaves may have been fed a small handful of uncooked crushed corn and brown sugar that morning. This close to the Apaches' home camps in the Chiricahuas or Dragoons, they would go on into the night to get home, even though they hated darkness.

The Apaches brought home treasures: cloth, coffee, brown sugar, flour, rice, beans and later gold coins and silver, too. Many of the best horses in the northern states of Mexico came on this road under the rein of a proud Indian boy turned man, a streak of black war paint and some red slashes across their faces. Scathing Apache raids made the north half of Sonora uninhabitable—abandoned ranches loose maverick cattle and horses roamed the land. And even with most of the Chiricahuas Apaches imprisoned in Florida, the spell they cast on the land prevented many returnees. So some bandits used the empty ranches to smuggle tequila and mescal across the border without paying U.S. customs fees. They soon replaced the Apaches and roamed the land, pilfering and raping the innocent at will.

El Maldito was one of the many gang leaders who had risen to powerful heights in this region. He paid off enough Sonoran officials to keep himself from being run down by what little law there was in the land.

"Why did *you* not take a posse after them?" she asked from behind him, beating her horse to keep him moving.

"Those men from town would die out here looking for nothing."

"I suppose so."

"Trust me, posses made up of townspeople don't last long in the saddle, especially down here in the Sonoran Desert."

She made a face showing she knew that. "How far ahead are they?"

"Ask the Apaches tonight. I waited a while to leave because

I figured if we made lots of dust they'd run like a prairie dog for their hole."

"I wondered why they waited a day to send you. I was getting mad that they got away again. Who are your Apaches?"

"Probably White Mountain. The Chiricahuas good and bad are gone."

"Maybe they won't cut my throat in the night." She gave a visible quake of her shoulders.

"Maybe," he agreed and sent the roan down the winding trail that descended into the Santa Cruz bottoms. Far to the southwest, he could see the line of green cottonwoods making a serpentlike track to the north, lining the water course. "We'll camp down there."

"Good. This stupid horse was not worth even stealing."

"You stole him?" He turned in the saddle to look at her. From the look on her face, he could see she didn't want to tell him much more.

"No. Worse than that. I borrowed him from my brother-in-law, Enrico's brother, Phillipe . . ." Then under her breath, she swore. "Such a *bastardo*."

"How much did he charge you?" He had to turn the other way in the saddle to see her red cheeks. She was shaking her head so hard, the long black hair fell in her face. She waved him away and motioned for him to go on.

"He sent his dumb wife to her mother's and made me sleep with him last night."

"Oh."

"Don't you tell anyone. I was so embarrassed, but I knew a burro would never keep up."

Slocum scowled at the sorry horse. "I real think a good burro would have beat him."

"He sure wasn't worth putting up with Phillipe all night, that is for sure. I feel sorry for my sister-in-law. He says, 'Am I like my brother in bed?' I wanted this damn horse so bad I bit my tongue. He is worse than a pig in bed—oh—"

"I heard a shot." He turned his head to listen for the next one. "Follow my tracks, but be careful. I'm going down there to see if my men are in trouble."

He sent the roan flying off the mountain. In places, it slid on its butt down the steepest part, scrambled for footing; then he used the trail, making the switchbacks and finally burst out on the flat. What could have happened?

Slocum stood in the stirrups, racing across the flats and tried to see beyond the rolling brown grassland. The line of cottonwoods grew closer. He noticed some gun smoke drifting away from a place in the tree line. What in the hell had happened?

Then he spotted three riders in sombreros shagging for the border. His roan was lathered and breathing hard. He had no intention of going after them with that large of a head start. He reined up short of the pack outfits.

Roy was carrying a smoking rifle and Sid stood holding the leads to the mules.

"What in the hell happened?" Slocum stepped off the sliding roan with his six-gun in hand.

"Guess they were waiting for us," Roy said. "Tried to jump us for the mules. We shot one of them."

Slocum could see the fine sorrel horse under the Mexican saddle grazing close to the river. Some rich rancher was sure missing a fine animal. He holstered his gun and went to where the groaning man in the brocade vest and chaps lay in the sand.

"Mother of God, have mercy—"

"Who are you?" Slocum demanded, down on his knee beside him.

"Benito . . . Morales . . . I am dying." He used one hand to squeeze Slocum's arm, the other bloody one he held to his stomach.

"Who do you ride for?"

"I am—"

"Listen, if you don't want more hell than that bullet, you'd better answer me. I've got Apaches that can skin you alive."

"El Maldito."

"Where's he at?"

"He was in our camp, but he left . . . Fronteras . . . his ranch . . . the Madres . . . I don't know."

"Think hard, hombre." Slocum listened to the man's spur rowels as he tossed and turned his boots in his pain. "Who sent you after my mules?"

The man shook his head. "We . . . found them . . . going home."

Like he had suspected. Happenstance.

"Why did you not go home with the others?"

"He said we were to watch and see if the posse came—"

Slocum shook his head in disgust and rose to his feet. El Maldito would know by dark about them—no way to stop them. Maybe his Apaches would return with some information. Fronteras and the Madres. It was a vast amount of land to cover.

"What about his horse?" Roy asked.

"Catch him. Mary will need him to ride."

"Mary?"

"The one trailing us will be here in an hour. She definitely needs that horse to ride. You will see."

"What's she look like?" Sid asked with slow grin.

"Good enough," Slocum said and went to loosening his cinch. "And I think she can cook."

"Boy, that'll sure beat having Roy do it." Sid chuckled and the shorter one went to hitting him with his hat,

The panniers had been set off, the mules and the horses watered and hobbled, when Mary finally appeared on the horizon, beating the fire out of her horse.

Sid nodded in approval, coming back to camp with an armload of wood. "She sure needs that sorrel all right."

"What happened?" she demanded, slicing the sweat off her face and bounding off the wind-broke, huffing horse.

"Maldito's men tried to steal the mules. Boys got one of them."

"Where is he?" She searched about in panic.

"Down there." Slocum indicated, busy building a fire in a ring of rocks.

"He dead?"

"No."

Before he could stop her, she stalked down the sandy bank toward him. Seeing the anger in her, Slocum dropped the twigs in his hands and started to follow her.

"Did you shoot my husband?" she screamed at the prone man. "Answer me! Answer me!"

Slocum began making a run in the sand. He could see she already had him by the vest and was shaking the fire out of him.

"Answer me! Damn you!"

"He's dead," Slocum said, on his knees beside her. "He can't tell you anything."

"The sumbitch—dying before he told me . . ." She released him with a look of disgust.

Slocum helped her up. "You can't do nothing about him now."

Her brown eyes narrowed in hate. "I would have cut his dick off."

"Sorry, his name was Benito Morales." He waited to see if the name struck her.

She shook her head. Then she began to cry. He hugged her and she buried her face in his vest. "They gunned him down for no reason. I miss him so."

"We'll get them."

She threw back her face. It was wet with tears, and she looked at him. "And I will help you get them. What can I do?"

"Sid won't brag on Roy's cooking."

She turned and for the first time noticed the two cowboys. Both had their hats off and held out a hand to her. She stepped over and shook their hands. "I will be your cook."

"We couldn't be prouder," Sid said and got an elbow in his side from Roy.

"Nice to have you here, ma'am."

On his haunches, Slocum bent over and worked on building the fire. "And they have a fine sorrel horse for you to ride tomorrow."

"Sure do. See that red one grazing down there?" Roy pointed it out.

"Oh, *si*. Such a fine horse. *Gracias*."

When they went after more wood, she joined Slocum.

"Such a fine horse And—" She looked around to be certain they were alone. "And I didn't have to go to bed for it."

They both chuckled.

4

Alone, Joe rode back to the camp at dark. Slocum frowned at his appearance.

"Where are the others?"

"They are watching those bandits who are camped at a water hole. Dio says they are the smugglers, too." The two men squatted in the twilight away from the camp and talked.

"Part of Maldito's gang?"

The scout nodded. "He says they are the ones who did the killing."

"They tried to ambush the cowboys today. Boys shot one of them. He told us Maldito had them wait and see if a posse came after them."

Joe nodded. "We have some more of them ahead."

"Those other scouts have food to eat?"

Joe nodded.

"Mary, bring Joe some food."

"*Si*, only one?" she called out.

"Yes," He turned back the Apache. "We may ride down there and jump them at daylight. Then they couldn't tell their boss anything about us. What do you think?"

Joe nodded. "Be plenty good idea."

Slocum knew that Apaches hated to prowl at night. But if they were ready to surround the camp at sunup that would probably work.

Mary brought Joe a plate of food. The Indian bobbed his un-blocked hat in gratitude and sat down cross-legged on the ground. "Damn. Good idea you get squaw."

"You saying I can't cook?"

"No. Good idea, you get her."

"Yeah, our bellies will appreciate her anyway."

"What do we need to do?" Roy asked, coming over.

"Saddle some horses. Take your bedroll. We may get a few hour's sleep. The scouts have some of the killers located."

"I'd like to get my hands on them."

"Sunup, you may get your way." Slocum rose and went to where Mary was washing dishes. "I've a sawed-off shotgun and a small pistol I'm leaving with you. All goes well, we'll be back midmorning and then move camp into Mexico. Only reason to shoot is to save your life. None of this plunder is worth dying over."

"I savvy," she said, sounding serious.

"You'll be fine. The smugglers are all in Mexico. Some camped down the way twenty miles. The rest farther down."

"I understand. Sorry, I lost my head at a dead man today."

"You were entitled to do that."

"I'll get braver about it. Right now his death stabs me right here." She pointed to the deep cleavage glowing in the orange light of the fire.

"Time heals many things," he said. "We'll be back." Then taking the roan's reins from Roy, he swung in the saddle. "That shotgun is in my bedroll. So are the shells. Make yourself at home in it." He swung the horse around. "Pistol is, too, and it's loaded."

She followed along beside his stirrup. "I'll be fine."

"Counting on it. These guys hate a man's cooking." Then they set out into the inkiness of night.

Joe finished eating his tortilla-wrapped food in the saddle, leading the way under the bright stars. The open grassland swept southward and spread out illuminated by the half moon. Slocum was anxious to at least get some of the killers rounded up. This might be a good chance to get El Maldito's best men and that would make getting the others easier and eventually the big man himself. Slocum twisted in his saddle and looked back toward camp in the starry night. His biggest concern was whether Mary would be all right.

Two hours later, the other scouts met them and fell in. Dio explained that four men were camped at a small spring in a side canyon.

"Is it open there?" Slocum asked.

The scout shook his head. "It's a steep canyon. Only one way in and one way out."

"Can we surround them?"

"Oh, *si*, senor."

"Good, we'll do that." Slocum listened to the footfall of hooves, the creak of saddle leather and the jingle of spurs. An occasional horse's snort punctuated the night.

Far short of the killers' camp he dispersed his men. The Apaches were to come in from above and cut off that route of escape. Slocum, Roy and Sid were to cover the front and try to capture their animals. Loose horses always went home and he wanted no clue to get back to their boss about what had happened to these men.

Sid slipped out of the saddle and jerked out his Winchester. "Guess this beats the hell out of that damned jail. But it's about to get serious, ain't it?"

"All of that," Slocum said and finished hobbling his horse. He could see the outline of the small mountain looming above them. According to his scouts the men were up this draw at a spring.

"Some whiskey might help right now," Roy said as he finished hobbling his pony.

"No, no little bit either," Sid said and shook his head ruefully. "I guess they'll fight."

"They'll fight. But not for long. Take off your spurs. We need to get up there." Slocum hung his own pair as well as his chaps on the saddle horn. Didn't need any noise or something to slow him down in case he had to move fast.

The oily Winchester in his grasp, he led the way. A few hundred yards, he discovered the sleeping horses and spoke to them softly. He and his men removed the hobbles without more than a few whispers. Slocum sent Roy down the canyon with the four animals so he could put them with their horses. Capture of the mounts made Slocum feel good about the operation since that would cut off any chance for the outlaws' escape.

Slocum hid behind one boulder, and Sid by another. They

could barely see the forms on the ground of the three sleeping figures. Three? Hadn't Dio said four men?

"Go back a hundred feet," he said close to Sid's ear. "Keep your back to the wall and watch out. One of them isn't up here. He may try to come up from our back side."

With a nod, Sid agreed and eased himself back down the brush-choked canyon. Slocum watched him slip away, then dried his palms on his pants. It would be light soon. He could hear someone coughing in camp. Probably stirring around, he decided. Slocum climbed higher for a better look.

The pinkish cast on the saw-toothed horizon began to glow behind them. He found a waist-high, flat-topped boulder and could view things better from up there. Still, he could only count three men in camp. One was up venting his bladder.

"Where is Cortez?" the man asked another in Spanish.

"He is like the wind and has gone somewhere."

Satisfied there was enough light to keep track of them, Slocum shouted. "You're under arrest. Don't move or you'll die."

"What?"

The warbling war cry of the three Apaches echoed in the canyon.

"Who are you?" one of the bandits shouted.

"Get your hands up or die."

"You're a gringo. But, but these Apaches—"

"Better mind them," Slocum shouted as the scouts moved in and disarmed them.

With his Apaches in control of the situation, Slocum started down the hillside to join them, avoiding beds of prickly pears. A shot rang out and he whirled. Damn. Sid was in trouble.

"Hold them," he shouted to the Apaches. He began to run once he reached the rocky trail. He hoped the shot had warned Roy farther down. On his boot heels running was hazardous. Turn an ankle or fall. He spotted a prone body in the path. Sid. He began to search the steep slopes above him illuminated by the bright sunlight high up on the brown and red pipes that accordioned the walls. No sign of anyone up on the talus-piled slopes. Then, more shots.

Damn, they were at the horses. He knelt for a second beside

Sid, but he could see the glaze over his eyes. Nothing he could do for him. More shots and then the drum of a horse leaving. Had the bastard killed Roy, too? A good plan had gone awry. An Apache on this end of the canyon might have detected the shooter as he came past.

"Roy?"

"I'm all right. Just got a scratch. He come out of nowhere. Everyone one else all right?"

"No, Sid wasn't that lucky. He back shot him."

"Aw, hell. That was my best pard." The cowboy collapsed on the ground holding his arm. Seated in an upright position, he dropped his chin and shook his head in sorrow. "Best one I ever had."

"I guess he never gave him a chance."

"Bastard—"

The Apaches were driving out the other three outlaws. Slocum made them sit on the ground and nodded, knowing he'd have to go back up there and get the body. Apaches hated even handling the dead. Women did that in their camp. The three grumbling pistoleros didn't look that tough, bare-headed and disarmed in his custody.

"What is your name?" Slocum asked the oldest outlaw.

"Vega."

"You work for Maldito?"

"Go ask him." He laughed openly and then he elbowed the other two for them to react.

Slocum made two swift steps, jerked the man to his feet by his shirt and punched him hard in the gut. The outlaw gave a great grunt, then he began to gasp for air.

"You think killing my man is funny? Wait until I get through with the three of you and see if you want to laugh. Do you work for Maldito?"

Coughing his life away, the man raised a hand in surrender. "*Si*, senor."

"Who's the man who killed my man and escaped?"

"Ramon Cortez." The man coughed some more, doubled over.

"Who's he to Maldito?"

"His brother-in-law. Married to Maldito's sister."

"What's her name?"

"Arana."

"The spider?"

The man nodded. "She is a *bruja*, too."

"Arana, the *bruja*. I'll stay clear of her web."

"Don't be so sure. She is more crafty than her brother."

"How many men were with the pack train?"

"Seven." He shrugged.

"Where will they go?"

"To Maldito's hacienda."

Slocum looked at Joe and the Apache nodded he knew where that was located.

"Tie them up. I'll go and load Sid's body."

"Can we bury him across the line?" Roy asked. "I'd not leave an old pard down here."

"Fine, you and one Apache can do that, plus take these three back to Arizona. The rest of us will go on."

"But that'll only leave three of you against all of them." Roy looked through his wet eyes at the others standing around him.

"We'll make it," Slocum assured him. "You've done your part. You can collect the reward on them, ride on and find some work."

Hat in his hand, Roy combed through his hair. "Where can I join you again? I want the bastard that killed my pard."

"Seeking revenge will get you killed."

"I'll find you."

"Be careful doing it," Slocum said and started up the canyon with Sid's horse. Cortez had stolen Roy's pony in his flight. But there were others for them to ride from the gang's bunch. Joe went with Slocum into the canyon, which surprised him. The Indian even helped lay out the blanket to wrap Sid's body in and then assisted in loading and tying the limp corpse over the saddle. One long day's ride and Roy'd be back in Bisbee. Maybe they'd have the others captured in a few more days. He hoped so, he thought as he led the pony back to the others.

His count was four of the gang rounded up or dead. Lots more to go.

In camp, Mary quizzed the prisoners hard about her husband's murder. But they all acted like they knew nothing. When she came back from talking to them, she kicked the pannier beside where Slocum squatted and frowned at him. "All of them are lying dogs. They know who killed him. Why do you waste time on a trial? I would personally shoot them in the back of the head."

"Holden is paying us to bring back prisoners. Tomorrow he will get some."

"I see."

"We may not be so generous the deeper we go."

"I savvy." She went for the coffeepot and refilled all their cups. "Who is taking them back?"

"Roy and Dio. You wish to return with them?"

An emphatic head shake answered him. "Who is this Cortez?"

"Another pistolero. He's married to Maldito's sister, Arana."

"You know her?"

Squatting on his heels, Slocum shifted his weight to the other leg. "No. They said she's a *bruja*."

"Are you afraid?"

He shook his head to dismiss her question. But, in truth, he wondered about a woman said to be so powerful. Many witches in Mexico and the southwest could foresee the future and put bad curses on people. All had varied skills, each excelling at different things. Some could cure ills with medicine they gathered; others used their power to destroy.

That evening he turned in early and was up before dawn helping Roy. Sid's body was rewrapped in canvas and bound with rope. The outlaws' hands were tied to the saddle horn and loops around each neck connected them to the same lead as the first horse. Dio was to ride as the guard. After a quick breakfast, Dio and Roy trotted off to the north with their entourage, promising to catch up with Slocum later.

Slocum, Joe and Black Wolf were left to load the mules. The job was not easy; the mules tried every trick in the book. Black Wolf dodged many heels thrown at him. He'd make a good hand, Slocum decided, noting the Indian's youth and agility.

With Mary helping, the loading was finally complete. When Slocum stepped into the stirrup, he knew one thing for certain, he'd miss those two cowboys turned mule skinners. Joe took the lead and Mary rode beside him with a quirt. Slocum sent the boy ahead to scout the way. The smile on his bronze face was enough—to be trusted for such work was an obvious privilege for him.

Two days later they reached La Linda, a small walled village with a well. Black Wolf reported the pack train had moved on from there the day before. It pleased Slocum to know they were within a day's drive of the killers. Perhaps Cortex was with them. He wanted him for the death of Sid.

All his senses aware, he sat in in the saddle and watched closely when his mule train came through the gate and up the street lined with the adobe walls of businesses. His hand on his gun butt, every muscle in his body was tensed. A few women washed clothes beside the well and they looked up when Joe brought the string of mules up to the watering trough.

Some individuals came out on the porches lining the square to observe the invaders. Slocum looked for any signs of a threat. Black Wolf was carrying a new rifle; he sat his horse on the other side of the well. Even Mary bore a long gun. Her eyes formed slits to see anything that looked out of place.

"Ah, senor." A portly man in a suit came from the cantina. "Welcome to La Linda." He swept off his sombrero and made a bow. "We are so glad to see you. May we stable your mules and have a fiesta tonight in your honor?"

"Those hombres that were here last night, did they have a fiesta?"

The man held his large hat before his chest and posed a sad face. "No, senor, but they were not men of honor. They raped a small girl and would not pay for their drinks."

"You know these men's names?"

"I could get them. Why?"

Slocum dismounted and after a check around nodded for the others to do the same. "Those men killed one of my men also."

"Bad hombres, senor. I will get their names from the bartender."

"Will twenty pesos buy a fiesta?'

"Oh, *si,* senor. Not a *grande* one, but it will be good."

"Is there a place this fine lady may clean up?" Slocum indicated Mary.

"Si." Then the man turned to one of the washerwomen and in a flash he told her to take Mary and help her.

The buxom woman grinned big at Slocum. "She will look like a new flower, senor."

Mary said she would see him later and hurried after her.

"Okay, *gracias*," Slocum said after her and turned to the other two. "Take the horses and mules to the stable. One must stand guard."

Joe nodded that he would take care of that and started to the stable. Black Wolf stuck his rifle in the scabbard and gathered the other horses. Slocum turned back to the man.

"Mayor, where may I get a bath?"

"Ah, come with me, senor. As my special guest I will see you are well taken care of."

One more check around the square and Slocum followed the man across the street. The mayor entered the doorway and clapped his hands. In moments, three young women dressed in loose-fitting garments came into the hallway beyond the front room and rushed forward. They nodded to the official.

"Our special guest, the senor, needs a bath and some kind care. He is providing the fiesta for tonight."

The brunette swept the hair back from her face and smiled. "Come this way, senor. The water will be ready in a few minutes. I'm am Estria, that is Mona and this is Ina."

Mona and Estria each grabbed an arm while Ina, the Indian girl, pushed on Slocum's butt as they took him down the hallway to the last room where a great copper tub waited. With great precision, they began to strip him of everything, including his gun. Mona rebuckled the holster and hung it on the post of a straight-back chair with a glance at him to be sure that its position met with his approval. Estria removed Slocum's vest and her hands moved over his chest and muscle-corded belly as if testing what was beneath the pullover shirt. Hat removed, she lifted the shirttail and he bent over to accommodate her.

Ina's small hands hugged him from behind. She pressed her rock hard nipples into his back as she undid his belt then the buttons of his fly. For moment, she squeezed the growing erection beneath his underwear and laughed aloud.

"Ah, *grande*."

He toed off his boots and Mona picked up his pants as he

stepped clear of them. Estria brought in two pails of steaming hot water and the Indian girl rushed after more. Button by button, Mona, the shortest of the three, undid his one-piece underwear. Her nimble fingers felt like the wings of a small bird touching his skin as she parted the material and forced it off his shoulders. The top half off, she pulled the rest of it down below his waist; then her eyes flickered when she saw his rod.

On an impulse, she hugged him. "Such a wonderful tree."

He bent over and kissed her. Then he gathered her up in his arms and their mouths spoke of fire.

"Let him bathe," Estria said and pried them apart.

Mona acted shaken and staggered back two steps. "Who cares?" she said dreamily.

Slocum winked at her and then stripped off the rest of his underwear. Standing naked for their inspection, he smiled at them and stepped in the tub. Hot!

Estria tested the water with her hand and spoke up, "Quick before we roast his *huevos*; get some cold water."

The pail in her hand, Ina rushed to get some cold water. The fiery heat soothed the tight muscles in his lower legs and made goose bumps pop out on his arms. The Indian girl dumped the water in the tub and stood back.

He nodded in approval as he slipped down into the steaming bath. The women stripped off their garments. He soon faced three naked women armed with soap and brushes. Their nearly black bodies hovered over him. Pear-shaped breasts swung in his face and tight small ones pointed at him.

Estria, on her knees beside the tub, lathered his face. Then with obvious skill, she cut away a week's beard growth while the other two waited for her to finish. Completed, she pursed her lips and kissed him, then rose to put away the razor.

The slender-bodied Ina stood on a chair with a pail in her hands and prepared to rinse him. Cold water cascaded over him as he rose. Then Turkish towels and vigorous hands rubbed him dry when he stepped out.

Estria shuffled a deck of worn cards and then placed them on the small table. "We will draw for first, second and third."

Mona reached over and disappointment showed in her brown eyes. "A damn seven."

Ina went next and her white teeth showed at the discovery of her draw. "A queen."

A pause and Estria's hand went to the stack and she picked up the top card. Her poker face held for a long moment, then she tossed it down. A five of clubs.

Ina took him by the arm and herded him for the door.

"One time is all you get, girl!" Mona warned her.

"We'll see," she said confidently and led him to the next room. Inside she drew the blanket curtain shut and turned to him.

He raised her chin and kissed her. Then his hand sought the rock hard small breasts as he hugged her to him. Viselike fingers closed on his partial erection and she began to gently jack him off.

"Let's get in the bed," she whispered and turned.

His hands caught her waist and he moved behind her. His expanding sword slipped between her legs. Bent forward she put her hands on the beds he moved his feet apart. She reached between her legs and guided the head of his dick into her moist gates. A cry escaped her lips when he gently shoved the rest of him deep inside. Then he began to drive in earnest. She hunched each time he drove it in her and the lips of her cunt began to swell. Their ragged breathing grew louder and louder.

Then she screamed and a flood of her juices ran out over his privates. He grabbed hold of her when she fainted. His dick popped out as he walked her limp form to the bed and eased her onto the mattress facedown. Almost immediately, he felt hands tearing him away from her.

"That little bitch can't take much," Mona said, pulling him after her to the next room. She dropped to her butt on the bed causing the ropes to protest and then moved like a crawfish on her back till her loose black hair was spilled on the pillow. Her short legs spread apart to show him the black thatch of pubic hair and pink lips of her moist pussy. With a curled finger, she coaxed him on the bed and into her den.

When he drove his throbbing rod inside her, her fingernails clawed at his back and in a smoky voice, she cried out, "Oh, yes."

Their pelvises soon crushed against each other and she began to grow more excited, crying out each time as his oversized erection began to rip her open with each stroke. She arched her back for him and her heels spurred a tattoo on his butt for more and more.

Then she began to strain underneath him. Faster. Harder. His butt began to ache to fill her full of fiery come. She began to cry out deep in her throat. He could feel the effort she made with her stomach muscles to get him to expel his charge. From deep in his scrotum came the cannon fire that rose like molten lead up the tubes and finally blasted out the overstretched head.

Mona collapsed in a pile. He found some space beside her. In seconds, his eyes closed and he fell into sleep, his body half-draped over hers.

It was dark when someone shook him. Estria put her finger to his mouth to silence him. "We have only a short time. Come, I need the same."

He stood and stretched, letting her lead him to the next room. After she closed the door, she walked over and began to ply his soft dick. His sword began to respond to her efforts and she smiled at her success in the candlelight.

"Let's get in the bed," she said. "Maybe he will get stronger inside of me."

Slocum nodded, knowing that what she had started would be hard to repress. She slipped off the gown and quickly was on the sheet with her arms held out to him. He crawled to get between her short legs. She moved down in the bed to be beneath him and with care shoved him inside her twat.

A smile began to cross her face and expose her white teeth as his erection began to grow.

"You knew he would," she said and closed her eyes as he worked to arouse her.

Larger and larger his circumference grew, and she closed her eyes and savored him. Then her fluid pussy began to respond. The lips thickened and her nail-like clitoris grew stiff enough to scratch his shaft. She let out a yelp and raised her butt off the bed, holding herself up with both hands, arching her back and crying out, "Yes! Yes!"

His throat ached from breathing so hard through his mouth. Finally, he came in a mad flood. Grasping both sides of her ass in his hands, he poured it into her until he was totally depleted.

"We've got to go to the fiesta," Mona said, shaking his shoulder to awaken him. "The mayor will kill all of us."

Numb-minded, he sat on the edge of the bed and nodded. "Let's go."

5

They left La Linda before the sun even looked peach colored over the saw-edged hills. Slocum's head hurt. Mica and Bigota were the mule tenders he hired the night before. Before they were loaded, the grateful Apaches left camp to scout ahead. Mica was a short, older man and Bigota, a boy of sixteen. Mica's younger cousin also assisted him. They acted like they knew mules and, in the noisy chorus, they worked swiftly and soon were on the road.

"You have any fun at the fiesta?" Mary asked. "I never saw you so done in before."

Slocum nodded from behind a pounding headache. "I'm fine."

"You look much better this morning. But I thought you were bad off last night when you showed up."

If three men screwed you to death, you might look the same, Slocum thought—but he kept his musings to himself. "Who was that guy you danced with?"

She shook her head under the straw sombrero. "Just a guy. I am not looking for one now. I want Enrico's killers first."

"I savvy that." He turned to be certain his pack train was coming. He could see them trotting to catch up. Satisfied, he turned back and looked at the wagon ruts in the ash-colored ground that wound through the knee-high greasewood and tall cactus.

"You have no wife?" she asked.

"No wife. Never been married."

"No home?"

"No home. The sky is my roof and the ground my floor."

She squinted out of one eye at him. "I can't imagine having no place that is your own."

"I have been like this for a long time."

"Don't you like women?"

He laughed. "I love them all."

"You have ignored me." She looked away.

"Oh, not on purpose. I've been busy. Besides you are in mourning."

She shook her head from side to side as if considering his words. "Maybe someone in my blankets would settle me so I could sleep."

"I accept your invitation," he said and took off his hat to her.

She blushed and looked away, pursing her lips. "Now you think I'm a *puta*."

"No—" He rode in close and kissed her on the check. "This will be our secret."

"Good." She sounded satisfied and a pleased smile crossed her mouth.

By nightfall, Black Wolf was back with a report. The packers, Joe thought, were pushing east for a place where they made mescal on the San Miquel River.

"Have they sold their stolen goods from Bisbee?"

"No, but Joe says they may sell them at this place and then head back for the border with another load of mescal."

"Makes sense. Could you tell if Cortez is still with them?"

The Apache shrugged. "We know the horse he stole from Roy is still with them."

"Where are they camped?"

"Joe said they are near the hacienda of Don Tomas."

Slocum scratched his cheek. They were within a half day of them. "Good, we need to catch them tomorrow and capture as many of them as we can."

"I will tell Joe."

"Be careful. They would kill you in a second."

"Ah, *si*." And the scout was gone in the night.

Mary came wearing a blanket against the night wind. "Are we close?" She squatted on her haunches beside him.

"Yes, tomorrow we'll get them."

"So soon?"

He nodded. "We'd better get some sleep."

She looked about in the starlit night as if to be sure that they were alone. "Those two are sleeping near the mules." She motioned her head toward the dry wash. "We could go up there."

"Good idea."

A smile crossed her face as if he had pleased her and she nodded. "I brought both bedrolls."

"We'll only need one, won't we?"

As if embarrassed, she put her face on his shoulder. "I never thought about that."

"Come."

The bedroll laid out, she sat upon it, took off her sandals and wiped the soles of her feet; then, fully dressed, she went under the covers. He toed off his boots and noticed how first she took off her skirt beneath the cover of the blanket and set it aside— all from under the covers. She exposed nothing but a bare arm that disappeared in a flash. His back to her, he undressed. When he turned to face her, he noticed her blouse was on top of the skirt and the covers were pulled up to her chin. On his knees ready to crawl in, he decided to offer her a way out.

"If you aren't ready for this, it can wait for another night."

"You won't be mad?"

"No, of course not."

"Good, I will try to get braver."

"That's fine," he said and flung out the other bedroll. In minutes, he was asleep. Some time during the night, the coyotes set up a chorus on the hill over them. In minutes, he found her form, fully dressed, lying against his back. He patted her leg and went back to sleep.

By dawn, the men had the mules loaded. Slocum explained to the pair that he would leave Mary with them later in the day. They were to make camp at a place called Grapevine and wait there for word. If all went well, he would meet them there the next day. "And if I don't return in three days, take her and the mules back to Bisbee. The man will pay you for their return."

"*Si*, patron," Mica said.

"You will be careful today?" Mary asked, concerned when the other two went to string out the mules.

He boosted her in the saddle. "Of course."

She looked around and then, with a grim set to her mouth, said, "I promise to be braver next time."

He grinned big. "I'll look forward to the time."

Rather than replying, she booted her horse on. He looked after her, amused, and swung himself up into the saddle. By dark, he should have most of the outlaws in his custody. He sent his roan after Mary and began to think about all he had to do.

By midmorning they parted. Mary rode with Mica and Bigota toward the spring at the old vineyards. After giving her a quick kiss, Slocum pushed east to find his scouts. Short-loping the roan horse, he pulled up at the flash of a mirror. Someone wanted him to know something. They were on the ridge to his right. He touched the gun on his hip, then sent the gelding off through the cactus and greasewood. Approaching the sheer face of a hundred-foot-high bluff, he wondered if the cut was the way for him to get up there.

No sign of his men. Strange they didn't appear. Then two shots rang out. The first bullet knocked him out of the saddle. Hit hard, lying on the ground, he saw other bullets strike the dirt and gravel around him, sending up a cloud of dust.

A trap. Damn, where were his Apaches? He could only lie still and hope the bushwhackers rode on and did not check on him. In the distance, he heard men arguing in Spanish, but the words were too distant to make out. He also knew only one thing else—blood was coming out of the wound in his side.

6

His greatest fear flashed in his mind as he tried to raise up from the acrid-tasting dirt—to die in the middle of some bad nightmare. His head swirled and he wondered about his fate. The sun was going down. Obviously the men who'd shot him were long gone off the escarpment. He could barely find the strength to sit up and then his vision would not focus. Where was his horse?

He was uncertain he could even stand, let alone muster the strength to mount the roan if he found him. Damn, he needed to get on his feet. The fire in his side made him clutch at it as he rose with care to his knees. The whirling in his head distorted his balance when he found himself standing, shaky at best. He tried to look for the roan. No sign of him. Maybe they'd stolen him. Lead-footed, he staggered a few yards. Holding his wound, the blood soon dried on his fingers and made them stiff.

Exhausted, he finally reached the wagon tracks. Which way to go—back toward the west? Or go east? Standing on rubber legs in the twilight, his decision-making ability was fogged by loss of blood and the pain. Which way should he go?

No horse. Nothing worked. Uncertain which way the horse went, Slocum staggered off until he fell facedown. He woke up in darkness. He could taste the acrid dirt again on his tongue. Was he eating it? Then the lights went out once more.

He recalled hearing voices talking in Spanish. "—is the

41

gringo alive? I don't know . . . maybe he is breathing . . . he's been shot . . . who did this? I don't know what to do."

"Load him in the wagon," a sharp voice of authority said.

"But what if—"

"What if what?"

Slocum awoke on a pallet in the back of a wagon. He could feel where someone had bandaged his wound. All he could hope for was they knew what they were doing. The next bump in the road rocked him back and forth. The jar hurt him and he closed his eyes to shut out the pain.

It was no longer night, and the heat was rising in the covered wagon piled high with crates and wooden barrels. Where were they headed? No telling. Who'd treated his wounds?

Then he heard a woman's sharp voice. "Make the mules go faster. That gringo in the back needs to see a doctor."

The bumps grew rougher, but at least he knew why. Cringing in preparation for the next blump in the road, he rode on the blanket bed they'd fixed for him. The weathered, brown canvas top shook on the bows overhead.

Time passed and he knew it was late, for the sun shone in the back oval of the wagon. Then the mules halted and he heard footsteps. A woman swept the black hair from her face and looked hard at him.

"At least you are still alive," she said, sounding relieved. In a few seconds, she pulled herself up and climbed over the tailgate boards. Lifting her skirt, she knelt beside him and held a canteen to his mouth.

He choked, but was grateful for the cool water in his dry mouth. She shook her head in his face and the long hair fell down. Forced to set down the canteen, she threaded it back and tied it with a rawhide string from her pocket. He guessed her to be in her thirties, slender body, but very strong. High cheekbones, diamond eyes and a thin mouth, not pretty, but not ugly either.

"Can you talk?"

"I guess," he said in a coarse gravely voice that shocked him.

"My name is Elainia."

"Slocum."

"Well, who shot you?" Then she turned to answer a man's comment from outside.

"Where is he at?" she asked with a tone of irritation.

"Gone to deliver a baby."

"We need to move him inside," she shouted to her companion and began to remove the top board of the wagon's tailgate.

"Carry him?" the man asked, sounding upset.

"How else will he get inside?" She shook her head setting the first board aside.

"I will find someone to help us," the man said.

She looked at the sky for heavenly assistance. "The gringo is only one man to carry."

But obviously her man had gone for another one and never answered her. She took out the last board and turned back to look at him. "Who did this to you?"

"Banditos."

"Ah, that is all we have in northern Mexico these days. Killers, rapists and madmen." She shook her head in disgust. "Why were you here?"

"To catch some men who killed a storekeeper in Bisbee."

She nodded. "On a fool's mission, no?"

"One is dead, three are in jail up there and I have more to catch."

"Save your strength—" She hung out the back to look for him, then ducked back inside. "He is coming with some others to move you."

"Where do you go from here?" he asked.

"Dos Padres. You know the place?"

He nodded. A small village at the foot of of the Madres.

"We will open a store there."

"You and your husband?"

She laughed aloud and shook her head to dismiss his notion. "That is my dumb brother, Phillipe. My last husband died in a border whorehouse in a knife fight over some pussy."

He half raised up at the sight of the man and the three boys at the tailgate.

"Now be easy with him or he will start the bleeding again," she warned them. "Come see me some time, gringo, if you live."

"Oh, I'll live all right and I will be by to see you."

"Good, I like a man who knows what he wants and knows how to get it." She reached out and slapped Phillipe's arm. "Go easy on him."

"I am. I am."

They maneuvered Slocum to the back, then one got under each armpit. Two took his legs and they hauled him inside the adobe building marked Doctor Espinoza. A woman in her fifties wearing a stiff starched dress ordered them around until he was placed on a cot.

"Do you hurt, senor?"

"Some, but I am hungry as a bear."

"I better not feed you anything with a stomach wound. I can give you mescal or tequila."

"Good, I'll get drunk and won't care."

The liquor she gave him was powerful and made his nose drip. The lava flow ran clear down to his hunger-pained stomach. A second glass and he went off into sleep. He awoke to someone undoing the bandage and in the lamplight saw the face of a young man.

"You, the doc?"

The man behind the gold wire-rim glasses nodded. "You the wounded man?"

"I think so."

He smiled friendly-like. "I must remove that bullet. But you are lucky, I don't think it perforated your gut. I can't smell anything anyway that would indicate that."

"That's good news. What's the bad?"

"Oh, getting an infection or something going sour inside you. What did she put on the wound? Some kind of powder?"

"You'll have to ask her. I wasn't conscious."

"Was she a *bruja*?"

"I ain't sure. I was dying where they left me and she brought me here."

"I have seen powder they used to stop a broken horned animal from bleeding. Wonder if she used that on you?"

"I don't know, I was bleeding and it had stopped when I woke up again."

"She used something. I can see traces of it. I'd better get the bullet out. I'll give you some laudanum." The doc went and washed his hands. "Mother, give him two tablespoons. We will operate in thirty minutes."

The straight-backed woman agreed with a nod and went for

the painkiller. She returned and held his head up to administer it. "Do you have any last of kin I should notify, Mr. Slocum?"

"No, ma'am."

"Very good, have the second spoonful."

In a few minutes, the lights went out.

Slocum awoke in a bed with starched sheets. His hand shot to his sore side and he could feel the bandages. He hoped the doc was successful and his guts had remained intact. The gray-haired woman the doc had called mother stuck her head in the room.

"He said you could eat some soup when you woke up."

"Senora Espinoza, I'd love that."

She wrinkled her nose at him and then smiled. "You have never eaten Maria's soup."

"I'll take my chances." His head felt numb six inches deep and his side hurt like two mules had kicked him in the same place.

"I'll get you some. You know you are a very lucky man."

"Yes, I figured that when I came to and wasn't looking at the furnaces of hell."

"You can joke on the threshold of death even. My, my." She hurried off in her blue-checkered dress.

The soup made his taste buds come alive. Maybe he would live after all. He looked up at the senora. "You'd better brag on her cooking."

She laughed openly and waved him away as she left him to feed himself, but the effort to eat wore him out and after the last spoonful he soon fell asleep.

Days passed slowly. No word from his Apaches. He felt certain that Mary had gone back to the border. His lengthy recovery disappointed him to the point of depression. When would he be strong enough to leave this place? Had the killers taken out his two scouts? No word about anything came to him. No one he asked knew anything about Maldito. Or more than likely out of fear they didn't want to discuss it with him.

But he also knew the way folks passed things on in Mexico. A wireless Mexican telegraph had probably already told the bandit chief that the gringo his men had ambushed lived on. If so, the man would send more assassins to take him out. He kept the six-gun close by his bed. Every time someone came in to see the doctor, like a knee-jerk reaction, he raised up, closed his fist on the grips and listened until he was certain that person in the outer office was no threat.

"You have many enemies in this land?" the senora asked as she and the heavyset Maria remade his bed with fresh sheets.

"Enough." He sat in a stuffed chair that she had moved in the room for him to use.

"One I guess is enough."

"If he wants to kill you bad enough, yes, one is enough."

"It must be very difficult to ever sleep with such a threat." The senora bent over and tucked in her side.

"I sleep with one eye open."

"Hardly resting. Well, sit up for while in that chair, Senor Slocum. Maria is making more of your favorite soup for lunch—chicken rice."

Slocum smiled at the cook. Senora Espinoza hated chicken rice, but he didn't. The buxom cook winked back at him as she bundled up the old sheets. He'd decided it was a game the two played with each other. Alone again, he slumped in the chair. The notion of such soup was the only thrill in his life.

Then, suddenly, in the outer room, two coarse voices demanded to see "Slocum!"

So he dove for the pistol and came up with it cocked. His knees on the floor, he rested his elbows on the bed as the pain from his effort sent cold chills up his jawbone.

A big man with a huge Chihuahua sombrero filled the doorway. "Where are you, you gringo *bastardo*?"

The Colt in Slocum's hand exploded. Boiling gun smoke filled the room. A sharp ringing hurt his ears as the man collapsed. The two women screamed and Slocum knew the second man was getting away out the front door. In a rush, he was at the window, blasting at the fleeing outlaw. Hit or not, he rode away.

Out of strength, Slocum stood with his shoulder to the wall. The empty pistol was in his right hand at his side. The gun smoke in the room stung his eyes. Damn he hated that the other one had escaped. It meant more trouble for him.

"You've overdone yourself," the senora said and assisted him into the bed.

"Can . . . can you reload my gun?" he asked and collapsed on the sheet with a hacking cough from the acrid smoke; he had to bend over double from the pain it caused him.

"Of course," she said.

"Reload it then, please . . ."

When she woke him for supper, he started to get up, glancing at the Colt in the holster. Then he sat up and took the tray from her.

"It's reloaded—five shots, hammer on an empty one."

"Thanks. Sorry they came here."

"One of them won't shoot anyone else. The undertaker has him."

Slocum nodded. The SOB lived by the gun, he also died by the gun. "Who was he?"

"They say his name was Arnaldo Baca."

"Who does he work for?"

She looked disappointed and shook her head. "No one says."

"Someone knows. They aren't telling out of fear."

"Yes, Senor Slocum that is right, I would bet. Now eat your soup."

He couldn't remain there much longer. Tray in his lap, he could smell the sweet chicken aroma in the vapors from his bowl. Maldito would send back tougher men for the job the next time. Strength or no strength, he had to leave the elegant lady and her hospitality.

"I will," he said and smiled at her.

She started for the door, then turned back. "A few hours ago you shot a man. I know he needed it. Does that not bother you?"

"He came to kill me."

"I know that. But I am still trembling inside. You aren't disturbed or anything?"

"Yes, ma'am, I am. Now they know where I am at. I'll rest a lot less easy."

"You think others will come because he failed?"

He nodded.

"I have known many men in my life. But you are somehow so different."

He grinned big. "How is that?"

"You are civil beyond most and tougher than any I've ever met."

"My mother, bless her soul would sure be proud of the first part."

The senora laughed. "Indeed she would be."

Left alone to consume his soup, he considered his clothing, laundered and folded neatly in the straight-back chair. He would need to shed the loose-fitting white shirt and pants she'd provided him to wear in bed. Then he would need a horse to ride or maybe just a ride. It would save him falling off a horse. Dizzy-headed as he was standing up alone—a horse would be out of the question.

If he didn't move on, his life would be worth less than a ten centavo piece.

7

The wooden axle screamed and the wheels of the *carreta* rolled over every bump in the ruts. On a pallet, Slocum felt shaken to pieces as the docile oxen plodded along. Juan Toya was taking a load of blankets, some clothing and shawls to Dos Padres. Never in a hurry, this freighter provided cover for Slocum's escape.

But midday, when the quiet man stopped to let his animals graze a few hours and take a siesta, Slocum knew he could never have ridden a horse away from there. After all the rough ride they were only a few miles from the senora's fine care.

She had provided him with some clothing to wear so he'd pass for a Mexican on the road. She'd also found him a sombrero since he'd lost his hat when they shot him. Guardedly, she hugged him and he'd kissed her good-bye. Then, about to cry, she'd rushed from the room. Maria assisted him to the *carreta* parked in front. Even boosted him up inside the back. There in the predawn's dim light he left the town, the senora, Maria and the young doctor who was always out making house calls.

Juan shook him when the siesta was over. "Time to move on, senor."

Out of his sun-blinded eyes, Slocum looked for a second in disbelief at the man. He thought for a minute he should be in the room at the doctor's again. No, he was in the desert. Weak beyond belief, he dreaded the remount into the back of the *correta*, but

Juan had the steers yoked and was ready to go again, so he got in.

God forbid the slow pace anymore. In the wagon, he soon fell asleep again despite the painful sounds of the creaking axle and the unforgiving lack of suspension. His world of hell continued. Days passed like long years. He walked some by the fourth day to escape the bruising ride.

"You are getting stronger," Juan said politely as they marched to the oxen's plodding steps.

Slocum agreed, but his recovery was not fast enough to suit himself. "This place, Dos Padres, how long before we get there?"

"Maybe a week, maybe ten days." Juan shrugged his shoulders under his serape.

Slocum nodded he'd heard the man. He needed a horse. But he could see no horse available out across the heat-wave-distorted flat greasewood country that surrounded them.

It was close to midday when he checked the sun time. Soon they would stop and take their midday break. He could count on that.

Some riders came racing down the road. They shouted curses at *carreta* for being in their way and charged past on both sides of the wagon.

"Who were they?" Slocum asked.

"Banditos, I guess. There are many like them in this land. Lucky they didn't shoot at us."

"Lucky? What for?"

"They need no reason to kill anyone, senor. They are cruel men."

Slocum nodded. He had avoided eye contact with the riders, fearing one might recognize him. On foot and against such odds it would be foolish to expose himself. When he would chose the time and place of his fight. This was neither. He wondered about the missing Apaches and whether those two Mexicans had taken Mary back to the states. Only time would tell and this Maldito and his men must be up to lots of bad things above and below the border.

But before he could do anything about it, he needed his strength back. And he needed to know more about the Maldito gang. All things that required painstaking time without the keen eyes of the Apaches or any contact with the rest of the population. Maybe in Dos Padres he could find some help.

"*Mañana*, we will be in Cristo and can find a drink to wash the trail dust from our throats."

Slocum agreed that was something to look forward to. He mopped his sweaty face on his sleeve and replaced the wide sombrero. The broiling heat reflecting off the dusty ground was making him light-headed.

"I better get in the *carreta*," he told Juan, who nodded that he understood.

"You need some help?"

Slocum shook his head and stopped to let the rig pass him so he could climb in the back. He bellied up on the bed and soon crawled in amongst the blankets. Despite the ovenlike heat he fell asleep in minutes, too weak to do anything else.

They reached a small village built around a well. Several date palms rose above the jacals and small green patches of irrigated land stood out in sharp contrast to the bland desert. Juan drove the team to the well and watering trough. The grateful steers mooed and drank deep. Slocum looked around at the few fighting chickens scratching in their droppings. Two cantinas and a store. A few hip-shot ponies were hitched to a rack. The saddles on them bore no long guns under the stirrups, so they probably belonged to vaqueros and not bandits. Slocum washed his hot face with his kerchief.

A woman came from a jacal. She was short with a long sharp nose. Eyeing them suspiciously, she put her hands on her hips. Slocum knew she would have a small belly roll under the dress, he could see it. Her breasts were compact, but she tried to expose them with a low-cut blouse.

"You are hungry?" she asked.

Juan nodded for both of them.

"I have some meat, green chili and black beans. I could make some fresh tortillas."

"How much?"

"For what?"

"Meat, beans, tortillas."

"Oh," she said, inspecting Slocum some more. "Ten centavos."

"Make us some," Juan said. "We must put the oxen in the corral first."

"Park your *carreta* in front of my jacal. No one will bother it there." She pointed to the one she came from.

Juan agreed and looked at Slocum.

"Fine," he said in response. He was only trying to get to Dos Padres to regain his strength. Somehow.

The steers in the pen, Juan paid the boy five centavos for the hay they would eat. Slocum hardly considered it forage, more a straw-looking pile that was mostly overripe foxtail and cheat. A horse would cough all day on the foxtails in his throat if he ate any of it. But to old steers, it probably did not matter. They'd missed many meals in their lifetime and they never minded the source. They began wrapping their black tongues around it and swallowed it whole.

The woman's name was Sasha and she talked all the time. On her knees at the fireplace, she padded out corn tortillas with her brown hands, then deftly put them on a blackened sheet of iron over the fire.

"You know the banditos were here yesterday?" she asked.

Juan told her he had seen them on the road.

"Bad ones." She made a face, slapping out another tortilla.

"Yes, *malo* hombres," Juan agreed.

"You see them?" she asked Slocum directly.

"Si."

"Those bastards only paid me twenty centavos and then three of them fucked me."

"Only paid you twenty centavos?" Juan shook his head in disbelief.

"They were cheap. Those little pig-dicked *bastardos*."

"I agree," Juan said. He and Slocum sat cross-legged and waited for their meal.

Then she used her index finger like a screw and made a sour face. "I would ram a big knife in their asses like this, if I ever had a chance."

"Good thing for you, they were not hung like elephants." Juan laughed at his own words.

She snickered and winked for Slocum's benefit. "Good thing, huh?"

He agreed, realizing how hungry he really felt from smelling her food.

On wooden trays, she served them the beans and meat with her brown-flecked tortillas. At his first bite, Slocum was impressed; he had expected some pasty, bland or too-chili-pepper-hot-to-eat food. Instead, his first mouthful drew the saliva flowing past his teeth.

"You like?" she asked in his face.

"Mucho bueno," he said in approval.

That seemed to please her and she dropped back, squatted on her heels. "Where are you going?"

"With him," Slocum said and gave a head toss to Juan.

"He comes by here every month or so. He is a good customer of mine."

"I see."

She wrinkled her too long nose. "No, you have seen nothing yet. But I will show you something later."

"Good, I like to see things."

"Can you play a guitar?"

Slocum shook his head.

"No matter, Juan can play one." She scrambled to her bare feet in a flash of brown legs, white slip and dress. In minutes, she returned with an old guitar and her brown fingers began strumming it.

"There once was a wild vaquero," she sang in a high voice, "who lived in the wild *montés* and for a senorita did fall—"

Slocum nodded as she went on, shuffling her bare soles on the hard-packed floor and plunking hard on the catgut strings. In a larger place she would be sought for her music. Slocum knew she could sing a ballad and make a man's heart go out to her. She stole his with her music. Then she pounded the strings and sang of the wild red mustang stallion called Flame. In the firelight, she sang of a man who rode after a thundering herd, swinging a lariat above his head, charging through the billowing dust to loop the great stud's neck and capture him for his own. He and Juan applauded when she finished and made a curtsey for them.

"More music," Juan said.

She smiled as if pleased by their attention. "Now I sing about the river."

Full of her food and sipping coffee, Slocum turned his ear to the tale of a river bathed in the quarter moon's light and a woman's lover who comes to meet her. Of the fast-passing time,

their too-short tryst, the dear minutes in each other's arms, so
wild their love. Then the woman is alone on the river bank,
bathed in moonlight. And when the quarter moon rises again,
he never returns—never returns. So forever her ghost walks the
river bank in the quarter moon, searching for the love she lost.

For the first time in two weeks he felt stronger, sitting on the
ground listening to this crooner and wishing more could hear
her voice and the words of her songs. For the moment, he
brushed aside all his concern for the others and studied the
woman with her long, pointy nose and high cheekbones back-
lighted by the orange of the fire. In her graceful way of sweep-
ing and dancing as she played the cheap instrument, he saw a
beauty that few women possessed. This was not some back village *puta*, but an actress, an entertainer like a cut diamond in a
handful of common stones. She gathered all the light and then
reflected it back at them.

She took the strap off over her head and handed Juan the
instrument. "Play music, *mi amigo*, while I entertain your
compañero."

Juan nodded and looked at the strings, fingering the frets.
Then his strumming brought to life the hard charging chords of
Spanish dance. Slocum took her proffered hands and stood up.
Her eyes, like chunks of coal, were the ones of sirens and she
led him out back to a bed under a lacy paloverde. There she
swept his hat off and put it on the bedpost. He threw off the serape and she lifted the shirt to take it off. Once clear he removed the gun belt and toed off his boots Her calloused fingers
traced over the bandage.

"Does it hurt?"

He shook his head.

Then she untied the cord holding up his pants.

He lifted her blouse, revealing her small breasts in the
starlight. Stepping towards him, she nailed her rock hard nipples against his chest and began to massage his privates with
both hands. Her hot mouth worked over this chest as if she were
ready to eat him whole. She moved backward to sit on the bed
and pulled off his pants. Then she dropped to her knees and
lifted his rising sword to lick the underside of the head. Her actions sent lightning to his brain and she laughed softly. The hard
music of the guitar drifted out in the cooling night.

Despite the catch in his side, Slocum pulled her up and she rose like a dark image, shedding the skirt as she stood. There, in the weak light coming through the tree, he could see the roll of her belly and the droop in her once proud breasts, but it made no difference.

On her back and beside him on the bed, his hand cupped the stiff curled pubic mound and she sighed. Spreading her legs apart, she pulled him on top of her. Juan's strumming grew louder, faster.

He climbed over her legs and popped his throbbing head inside her wet pussy. She threw her head back and cried, "Yes."

He could see her windpipe and the cords in her neck as he plunged into pleasure's alley. How long since he'd been been taken to the doctor—two weeks? No matter. He wanted to send this singer to some bliss-filled land for her efforts to entertain him. Braced over her, he could see her boobs shaking as she arched her back to take in all of him and they moaned as they fought the war and sought the peace on the other side. Her contractions began like spasms, then a great vise closed in on his aching shaft. The music grew faster and faster. Then the swollen head of his dick exploded and she clung to him until she slipped into a faint.

The music stopped.

Before daylight, Slocum and Juan yoked the oxen and began the next day's journey. The woman stood in the doorway and waved good-bye to them in the purple light. Slocum fell in beside Juan who shouted at the ox and cracked his whip with authority. The cool temperature of the morning would soon be replaced with the brain-depleting fire of the noonday sun. The only music in Slocum's ears now was the screech of the wooden axle and the memory of the woman's stirring voice.

8

They arrived in Dos Padres, a village in the foothills of the Sierra Madres. The way there led over an arched stone bridge that crossed silver water rushing underneath. A dozen or more bare-breasted women knelt beside the stream washing clothes. Some hollered and waved at them. The road, laid in stones, swept past the small farms under the cover of towering, gnarled cottonwoods that hosted a million gossiping birds.

At last they were going up the one-sided business section that faced the small river's course. Some villagers came out to see them and wave.

"What did you bring?" a man in a white apron asked, wiping his hands on the tail of it.

"Blankets, serapes, the usual," Juan said to him.

"You should bring pretty *putas*, not things to wear." He kissed his palm then released it like a dove. "Who wants clothes anyway?" He shook his balding head as if disgusted no whores had arrived and went back inside his cantina.

"I will surprise him one day and bring him some," Juan said in disgust.

Then they both laughed.

"Who is this hombre with you, Juan?" Elainia asked, squinting at him from the high boardwalk above them.

"Ho!" Juan stopped the team. "You know him. His name is Slocum."

"Sorry," she said, coming down the slope in her high heel boots. "I did not recognize you in that clothing."

He removed his hat for her and bowed. "It's me."

"Good, but what all has happened to you?"

"It is a long story. I would love to tell you all about it but first I must help my amigo park his *carreta* and put up his team."

"No, I do it all the time by myself. Elainia will love your story."

"Come." She linked his arm with hers.

In surrender, he went without a fight up the incline to the boardwalk.

"Tell me, big man, what happened after I last saw you?" She led him though her small shop piled with goods. Out back under a lacy tree in the sunshine they sat on some cane chairs facing each other. He noticed the mole on her upper lip for the first time.

"After you left me, the doctor removed the bullet—" He began telling her and she listened intently with her brown eyes like chucks of coal focused on his every word.

"No sign of your scouts?"

Slocum stared off at the adobe wall that surrounded the patio and shook his head. The woman before him was in her thirties. Handsome, willowy figure and long brown fingers that she used expressively when she talked. A hands-on person, she reached over and touched his knee at times as if contact would make her words more powerful. Hair black as a raven's wing was piled on her head. Her tan blouse was made of silk, and it fluttered over her small breasts in the cooling winds off the mountains. Many petticoats showed when she crossed her legs, giving him sight of her boot tops.

"I am sorry. I heard lately that they killed two Apaches."

"They?"

"Maldito's men."

The knowledge of their deaths stung him like a bullwhip. In his mind when they did not return and find him, he had to suspect they were dead. But the knowledge of the fact cut like a knife in his heart. He owed them. They must be the toughest bunch he ever was up against—no one slipped up on men like Joe and Black Wolf. He'd better take heed.

"Where will you go next?"

"To find their killers."

She raised her face, looked hard at him and shook her head. "No, they will kill you, too."

"They tried that."

"They will succeed the next time."

Her hand on his knee again, she leaned forward to speak to him. "Listen to me. You would need an army to get to him. He is like smoke and blows away on the wind."

"You're saying he's a spirit."

"Worse than that." She looked around, then lowered her voice. "He's maybe the devil himself."

Slocum sat back, his side still sore. This woman was one who knew things, maybe not a *bruja*, but she was at the least a psychic. He must listen to her and learn all he could about his enemy.

"Go back to the States. There is no way to stop them. The *federales* tried, but he either bought them off or they are afraid of him."

More than likely he'd bought off the officials, Slocum decided. That was cheaper than fighting them. He felt so alone— no horse, no rifle, no money, no ammo, only an alluring woman to talk to in the midmorning sun.

"—my bad manners." She broke into his concentration.

"I'm sorry?"

"I didn't offer you a drink or food. My bad manners, I said."

He flexed his stiff shoulders and dismissed her concern. "Maybe a bath. Is there such a place I can get one here?"

"I have towels and soap. We can go a short ways upstream and you can bathe behind some willows in the stream." She gave a head toss toward the mountains. "The water is cold."

"No problem. What about your store?"

"An old woman, Mia, is here to wait on them. Besides they mostly come on Saturday to shop."

So they left the store with soap, blankets, towels, some beef jerky and two bottles of wine in a basket. She acted like a young girl going on her first picnic. Under the fluttering cottonwood they passed several small irrigated farms and went over a number of wooden bridges that crossed the small ditches that fed these places their lifeline—water. To their left, behind a screen of bushes, a stream gurgled over the well-worn rocks. She led the way from the road to a secluded spot where the grass was mowed short by grazing animals. Waving the blanket open, she spread it on the ground, then placed the items on it. He took off his hat and the serape. Elainia stepped toward him and he took her in his arms. Her lips set, she turned her head back and he kissed her.

Her body hard pressed to him, and he savored the honey in her mouth. Her small breasts feel like nails through the cloth of his shirt. The world tilted and he raised his lips from her mouth. "You have no man?"

"He died. He was old when I married him as a girl. But I loved him very much."

"And so he left you money."

"Enough, so I am not a *puta*."

"I understand."

"A woman is either a wife or a whore in Mexico."

"One is respectable even if she beds every man she meets. The other is suspicious, huh?"

He toed off his boots, listening to the noisy birds overhead in the rattling cottonwoods whose gnarled arms spread out over their glen. The dollar-size spinning leaves filtered out the high sun's rays while he undid his gun belt and dropped it to the blanket.

Seated on the woven cotton cover, her keen eyes never left him as he took off his shirt and undid his pants. He winked at her, turned away and shed his britches.

"That water is cold, hombre. Don't freeze it off."

"I'll try not to." Soap in hand, he headed for the inviting stream. At first, he drove into the cold water to his knees. The chill was heart-stopping for moment, then his body adjusted to the frigid temperature. He began to soap himself and looked back to her.

Hugging her knees, she was smiling like a fox waiting for the henhouse door to open. His mind was more on how to take this Maldito out than on what now lay on the blanket. Bad when revenge interfered with pleasure so much; it made him lose perspective. Not good when there was a willing body on the ground not twenty steps away.

Elainia reclined on her side, head propped up by an elbow.

He tossed the soap on the rocks and then dove in the cold water. Coming up, he tossed his too-long hair aside, grasped a deep breath and then jackknifed again under the roiling current. After all the heat and acrid dust of the desert, this stream felt like something heavenly. Clean at last, he waded for the shore and she stood ready with a large towel.

She began drying his back. Her hands moved swiftly as if in a hurry to complete the task. Then she spun him around and dried his face. The rapid evaporation off his skin caused goose bumps on his arms as she carefully patted dry his cheeks. Then she did the same to his chest with vigorous rubbing of her hands over his body underneath the towel.

On her knees before him, she began to dry his privates with dedicated care. The towel behind his scrotum, she brought them forward on her palm as if they were crown jewels. Sunlight danced on the droplets clinging to the coarse black pubic hair. Then her other hand began to pull on his limp cock. Soon she had the shaft in her fist and smiled up at him as if she had opened a Christmas package and found her greatest wish.

She popped the head of his dick into her mouth. Her lips closed around the ring. To steady herself, she gripped his legs as her tongue rasped the surface until Slocum stood on his toes to escape the thrill of her actions. Damn!

At last she broke loose and gasping for her breath, she pulled him down to his knees with her. "Oh, sweet Jesus," she huffed for air, looking dizzy with passion. "Take me now!"

On her back, she fought to pull up her skirt and layers of petticoats to expose her shapely legs. She raised up and looked down to see if the way was clear for his anticipated entry as he moved between her raised knees. When he shoved his rigid sword through her wet gates, she cried out. "Yes, yes, burn me down."

He tried to, moving forward over her so his dick soon rode against the point of her stiff clit. He felt the walls begin to tighten. She moaned with each pistonlike stroke. Every muscle in her butt ached to drive his force into her each time. Soon their swollen entities became so skintight, pain replaced pleasure and they fought harder and harder to escape it. He drove himself so deep, he drew a groan from her. Frantic for the end, her boot heels danced on the back of his legs. Then she arched her back, raised her butt off the blanket and he came like a mountain caisson going off—a full satchel of black powder charge sent the cannonball in flight. They collapsed in a spent pile.

"Where will you go next?" she asked, lying side by side next to him.

"I need a horse, saddle and rifle."

She closed her eyes and rolled on her back to look at the ceiling of fluttering leaves. "You will be killed."

"I die hard."

"Your enemy is a tough bastard. He hires only the toughest men."

"His hide ain't so thick a bullet can't stop him?"

She rolled over on her stomach and propped herself upon her elbows. "You don't understand. This is the meanest sumbitch I have ever known."

"He killed my scouts."

"Stay here and make love to me. Going after him will only get you shot again."

"I need a—"

Her fingers cut off his speech. "I will find you a horse, a saddle and a gun. Now—" She scooted closer to him. "Make love to me again."

Hours later, she returned on horseback and brought him a small blue roan with a line down his back and striped legs. A tough mountain-bred gelding, maybe five years old from Slocum's examination of the horse's teeth. The saddle was Mexican-made with a large horn covered by a shrunken bull's sac. The pads under the saddle looked thick enough to protect the pony's back from sores.

"You like him?" she asked, standing back, hands on her hips with a riding quirt dangling from her right wrist.

He turned and looked mildly at her. "What did he cost?"

"He is a gift."

"I didn't ask for charity."

"He is a gift."

"Fine, I'll put him and your horse in the corral. Thank you, he's a special horse."

"Good, I'm hungry. Let's have some food. Madonna?" she called out for her housekeeper as she removed her thin gloves, striding down the hallway. "I am home."

Over her shoulder, she added, A man will deliver a rifle for you tonight. "He had to go trade for it."

"How will I repay you?"

"Go back to the States and forget this call for revenge that is eating you up." She bent over and hugged the old woman at the fireplace and spoke to her in Spanish about her cooking.

"She says the goat is done." Elainia rose and straightened her back as if it were sore. "Now when will you leave?"

"Tomorrow."

"I thought so." She closed her eyes and shook her head in disappointment.

In two steps, he gathered her against his body, then kissed her mouth hard. When they took a breath, she looked up, her hat on her shoulders and nodded. "There's no sense in you dying."

He hugged her to smother away her words. He would get Maldito or else.

That evening, a man brought by a well-used Winchester, but it worked. Slocum spent the next two hours cleaning and oiling it. That completed, she came and led him off to her bed.

"I won't sleep well worrying about you," she said, lying beside him.

His hand massaged her right breast. The rock-hard nipple scratched his palm as it grew more pointed. "Sleep. I will be all right." Then his mouth found hers.

9

He left Dos Padres before the sun topped the mother mountains. The only thing he knew was the word he had learned from a stable hand. Maldito might be in the Sierra Madres near the Rio Blanco at a ranch he kept up there.

"Why is he up there?" Slocum asked the youth from the stable before he rode out of town.

"Even the *federales* don't go up there."

"Good reason," Slocum said and paid the boy ten centavos.

Midday, he found a small village and an old woman selling tamales. When he met her gaze, he suspected she had powers. He dismounted and hitched the roan to a rack. Then he came over to squat close by her.

"I am looking for Maldito. You know where he is?"

"If I knew, I would not tell you." She handed him a tamale.

"Why?" He peeled back the shuck wraps.

"If you asked me how to commit suicide, would I tell you how to kill yourself?"

"Why not?" he asked, enjoying the spicy meal from between the corn shucks.

"They would kill you before you even found him."

Squatting on his boot heels, he laughed. "Look in your wizardry and tell me if he is there and I will worry about staying alive."

She wrinkled her nose at him. "I have no wizardry."

"But you know if he is there." This old woman gave him crawly feelings and he knew she was a *bruja*. They knew of many things and if they felt generous would tell you what they knew, otherwise they'd ignore you.

She nodded and made a sour face at him. "Go and get yourself killed."

"There were two Apaches. Have you seen what became of them?"

"Yes." She looked hard at him. Her eyes were like two chunks of coal. "I see them facedown in a dry wash, somewhere. They both were shot in the back of the head."

"Gracias." He gave her three ten-centavo pieces. How had Maldito's men discovered the two Apaches? They were slicker at scouting than he would ever be. What chance did he have against such an outlaw? Only time would tell.

He took the winding tracks into the foothills, a way he knew eventually would take him to the Rio Blanco. Blue Sonora doves dusted and flitted on the road ahead of him. Their soft cooing sounded in his ears as he trotted the roan horse. At nightfall, he reached a small stream of fresh water and hobbled the horse. Then he took his blanket to a place where the rock outcroppings would make a good defensive shelter. Rifle over his lap, he chewed on some hard jerky. From then on, he would be on his own and have to be careful. Maldito knew he was on his way to find him. The shooter who had escaped at the doctor's had been a big mistake.

He heard horses coming. Suspicious, he rose and tried to see downhill through the junipers. An unblocked straw hat some Chinese coolie might wear came first and then he frowned at the second rider. It was Mary.

"Hello," he said to the older Indian in front and stepped out of his rock fort.

"You must be Slo . . . cum?"

"It's him, Chief," she said, booting her horse forward. "Have you seen Maldito?"

Slocum shook his head. "Why did you come back?"

"He is the boy's grandfather," she said. "They share the same English name even. I told him I'd help him find his grandson's killer. I can't pronounce his Indian name so I call him Chief."

Slocum shook his head in disappointment at her. "It's too dangerous for you to be up here." He turned and said to the Indian, "I am sorry about your grandson, but you're liable to meet the same fate up here. These men are killers."

"I don't care," the old man said in his sand-crusted voice. "San Carlos is a bad place to die."

"I agree. It's a hellhole."

"Where is Maldito's camp up here?" she asked, undoing the latigoes.

"Ahead somewhere on the Rio Blanco."

"I see. What did you have to eat?" She looked around with the saddle in her hands.

"Jerky. I didn't want a fire."

"You're right," she said, looking disappointed at his reply. The saddle set on its end, she straightened and shook back the hair from her face. "I was glad to hear that you were alive."

"I wish you hadn't came up here."

"I am here. Chief came and spoke to me about his grandson and how he feared what had happened to him." She headed for the pack horse and he followed her. "After I agreed to go with him to look for the men who killed his grandson, I went and spoke to the man at the mine."

"Duke Holden?"

"Yes, he's the one and I told him I wanted to go look for you. That I thought you needed help. He gave me the money for the pack horse and some supplies."

"I need fighting men."

"Not an old Indian and me?" She looked amused and stared at him as twilight descended.

"Right. I've lost two good men. Murdered by those cutthroats. This army of three doesn't stand much chance against them."

"Well, I found no takers that wanted to come down here. The mention of El Maldito's name was all it took. Oh, they would come and try to catch smugglers but no one would mess with Maldito."

"Sometimes, a few can do plenty," Chief said and a grin appeared on his chiseled brown face.

"I hope so," Slocum said and took the pannier off the pack saddle.

"Have you seen their camp?" he asked, squatting on his

heels to roll a cigarette. When Slocum shook his head, he said, "Tomorrow I will show it to you."

"Is it close by?" Slocum asked.

Chief nodded, struck a match on a rock and puffed on his roll-your-own. There, under a strange-shaped, flat-brimmed straw hat held under his chin by a rawhide strap, squatted an ancient warrior. Dressed in a wash-faded army shirt, a once white loincloth and knee-high Apache boots was a relic of the old days, with a thousand wrinkles and the battle scars to prove it. But his eyes were those of a twenty-year-old and his body a sinewy hard knot—too tough to kill and ruthless in pursuit. His purpose was clear to Slocum, he wanted revenge for Black Wolf's death.

Slocum was still impressed at how the old man knew about the camp. "You've been to this place before?"

Chief shook his head. "No, but I saw it in a vision."

"Good enough."

A small smile appeared at the corners of his thin mouth. "You have visions?"

Slocum shook his head and undid the other pannier to unload it. They were both heavy and that meant she'd brought them food and ammo.

"I've never had one, but I have had feelings good and bad about things before I rode into them." Slocum gave the pannier a boost with his knee and got a new grip on it to set it down. "This vision is a good one?"

"I think so for now," Chief said, then he puffed on the butt of his cigarette holding it between his thumb and finger.

For now? The notion the old man wasn't telling him all that he knew rolled over in his mind as he watched Mary hand some jerky to him. Then she sat down on a large flat boulder and began to chew on her own.

"I would have built a fire," she said between bites.

He nodded, studying the sun's last rays on the tops of foothills above them. "I just want to be careful."

"Can't be enough."

"Right. I worry about you being along." Slocum closed his eyes to the notion. He wished she hadn't came down there.

"I have nothing else to do." She looked at the ground. "I

want him dead for killing my husband. He was all I had." Then she raised up and shook her head as if to clear her mind. "Someone needs to try and stop him."

"We'll get him—in time."

She nodded and turned away.

He let her regain her composure. "We'll go look for them in the morning. You'd better take care of the horses and supplies."

"I can fight."

"There'll be plenty of time for that. First, we need to know where they are and see how many are with him. We'd better get some sleep."

She agreed and took the old man a blanket. He wrapped it around himself. Then nodding, he sat back down and chewed more on his jerky.

"You need more food?" she asked Slocum.

"I'll be fine. Keep an ear out for any sign of trouble," he said and went back to his own bedroll.

"Thanks, Slocum," she said quietly after him.

Dawn came like a soft purple glow on the peaks of the mountains. Slocum and the Apache laid on their bellies atop the bluff and watched the camp stir beneath them. The low smoke of cooking fires obscured some of the residents, but the ones up that Slocum could see were women preparing meals.

Chief elbowed him as a man came out and stretched. "There is the one called Squaw Killer."

Slocum studied the black-bearded man with his barrel-shaped body as he stood beside a walled tent. "Any sign of Maldito?"

The Apache shook his head, looking intently at the goings on beneath them. Then he gave a head toss at a second male. "That is a Yaqui Indian named Solomon."

Slocum could see the man had silver braids. "He an old chief?"

"No, him a young man. Hair turned white when they had him in prison."

"What for?"

"Murder—who knows."

"How many more men are down there I wonder?"

Wolf wrinkled his nose. "Not many. There are only a few ponies in the pens."

"Where's El Maldito?"

"Maybe Fronteras."

"Maybe anywhere," Slocum mumbled to himself in disgust.

"Huh?"

"Never mind. We need to take them."

Chief nodded. "We can move close from the canyon side. Got bad bear scent. Make their dogs piss all over themselves and go crazy when they smell it."

"Won't that warn them?"

"No, be too busy kicking them damn dogs." He chuckled.

They eased back into the timber and made their way south from the rim. Slocum carried the Winchester and the old man had a single-shot trapdoor rifle, two belts of ammo and a black powder six-gun in a holster on his hip. Plenty of arms, but they sure might need that much firepower. The pair in camp, Slocum felt certain, were not strangers to shoot-outs.

They worked down the canyon side, being careful they were not in sight of anyone in camp. The old man's route through the pungent-smelling jack pines and junipers was not an easy one. Slocum was amazed at his light-footed agility. They paused to catch their breath when a goat began to bleat at them.

Chief nodded as if pleased and whispered, "He will be our messenger. We must catch him."

Slocum scowled. Catch a damn goat? What for? But he kept his comments to himself. Crouched down behind a bushy juniper, he waited where the old man signaled he wanted him to stay put. His rifle and ammo belts set aside, Chief disappeared and soon returned with a small goat in tow.

The critter bleated a lot, but that did not discourage the old man. "Hold him."

Slocum obeyed, catching him by the scuff of the neck and muzzling off his complaints. Chief opened a buckskin pouch and then Slocum could smell the strong bear scent. *Whew*, it was powerful. The goat about went crazy when he caught the odor and tried to flop over on his back to escape it, but Slocum managed with both hands to hold on to the thrashing, panicked animal.

"Point him toward camp," Chief said and Slocum aimed him

in that direction while the Apache put something on the goat's butt.

"Let him go now."

Whatever he applied to the goat's ass must have been turpentine. He left out like a racehorse, bleating at the top of his lungs and was gone in a flash. Chief nodded in approval and put on his bandoliers and picked up his rifle.

The dogs in camp began to bark and whine like they'd gone crazy at the frenzied goat's arrival.

"Good, we'd better hurry," Chief said and they began to run.

Two yellow curs ran past them going the opposite way like the devil was on their tails. Slocum looked back, but they were gone howling as if they'd been shot. He and Chief rounded the bend and there were the two men kicking and stomping the other gone-crazy dogs.

Chief put the rifle to his shoulder and shot the one called Squaw Killer.

The Yaqui made a move for his own gun, but it was too late. Slocum dropped him with the .44/40. The women began to scream and run for cover. Chief started blasting dogs with his old Colt and the rest ran away. In minutes, the panic settled down. Frightened women and children came out of their jacals and lined up.

"Where is El Maldito?" Chief asked.

No answer. Only the suspicious dark eyes of four young women. An occasional child whined, then he buried his face in his mother's skirts. They were all *indios*. Not attractive, but obviously the kind to keep camp up there in the Madres.

"We shoot this boy," Chief said and grabbed a youth of perhaps five from his mother out into the dusty center of camp near the cooking fires. "Tell us where he is at."

His words echoed in the silence, save for the murmur of the wind in the pines.

"Don't kill Tomas, please—" a small woman pleaded, clasping her hands together.

"I will kill him, then another until one of you tells me the truth."

"Fronteras," another woman shouted.

"Where in Fronteras?"

"He has a casa there."

"What street is it on?"

While the chief was talking, Slocum knelt and turned over the two outlaws. It was clear neither would survive their wounds. With care, he moved around checking the jacals. Looking inside a small hut, he recognized a silver cross on a leather thong hanging on a wall inside. He stepped through the doorway, careful to look around first, and then he removed it from the wooden stick hook.

"Ask them whose casa this is?" Slocum said, ducking the lintel to come outside.

"That is El Maldito's casa. Why?" Chief asked, after interrogating the females some more.

"He hung this cross in it."

Chief holstered his Colt and took the cross. With care he turned it over and looked at it in his palm. "It was one my grandson wore."

"I thought so. I guess we'd better go to Fronteras and find his killer."

"What about the Squaw Killer?" Chief tossed his head at the prone man's body.

"He's dead."

"Good. He shot my wife and sold her scalp for ten dollars."

"The world won't miss him. Yaqui won't last till sundown."

"What will we do?" a sharp-faced woman asked.

"Live your lives," Chief said. "But if I ever find you in a bandito camp again, I will cut your throat." He made a slicing motion with the hand that held the cross and rawhide string.

The women moaned and hugged their children.

"You ready to leave?" Slocum asked.

"Yes, we ride two of their horses back to ours. No walk."

Slocum nodded, amused. Only an Apache would have thought of that—why walk when you can ride. Saddled and ready to go, Slocum carried a pearl-handled Smith and Wesson .45 he had removed—the holster and all—from the still body of Squaw Killer. Chief had a new cartridge model Colt in a gun belt slung over his left shoulder when they rode out.

An hour later, with a fat yearling mule deer tied over the outlaw's bay horse, they rode into camp.

"I can build a fire now?" she asked, looking wide-eyed.

"Yes, El Maldito was not there." Slocum nodded at her questioning look. "The main bunch is in Fronteras."

"Did you get some?"

"Two," he said, dropping heavily out of the saddle.

"Who were they?"

"Squaw Killer and a Yaqui with silver hair."

"Where's Chief?" She whirled around to look for him. "He all right?"

"Talking to his God up on the mountain. I found Black Wolf's silver cross up there. He'll be along," he said.

"Fine. So I can start the fire?"

He nodded. "And I'll skin the deer. He's fat."

"Good. Will Chief be all right?"

"Fine. One of the two dead men had killed his wife for a ten dollar scalp."

Upset, she shook her head. "He has many sad stories to tell about his people."

Slocum looked back up the mountain he had came from. No doubt that was so.

10

Slocum and his crew came out of the mountains and stopped at the village of Marsea. He did not want to use the same route to return upon as he used going in. That way they might avoid the gang members sent to ambush them. Little doubt that El Maldito wanted him dead by this time, even though he probably did not yet know about the attack on the mountain camp. So anywhere could be a trap placed by someone who wanted the bounty on his head. It was a problem he seldom had to worry about across the border; but now this outlaw chasing business had made him wanted even in Mexico. There was no sanctuary.

Marsea was a few hovels on a tan dirt hillside with grease-wood bushes for yard plants, a few palms and some precious acres watered by a burro-powered pump. The rest was desert, without even organ pipe or prickly pear cactus. A long, wooden tongue that a pair of donkeys pulled around and around was tied to the gears that in turn pulled the leather sucker rod jack up and down. The water spilled into a trough and then went down a tile pipe to the green acres of corn, melons, peppers and beans.

"Ah, senor." The man in white clothing removed his straw sombrero and bowed. "Welcome to Marsea, *mi amigos.*"

"Gracias, buenas tardes." Slocum dismounted and pulled his pants out of his crotch.

"What can I do for you?"

"We wish to water our horses."

72

"We get ten centavos for each one, senor."

"What does El Maldito pay you when he comes by?"

"Who is El Maldito, senor?"

Slocum shook his head. "You know the bandit boss. Don't lie to me. He pays nothing for this water."

"Ah, you must work for him?"

"Damned right, I do."

The man bowed, looking taken back. "Pardon me, senor. But the village is very poor. We must get all the money we can to keep the pump going or we will die of starvation here."

"We will water our animals and ride on."

"Certainly."

"Bring us some food and I will pay you." Slocum looked around and knew the Apache's sharp eyes had scrutinized the safety of the place. Satisfied nothing was out of place, Slocum helped Mary off her horse. "You making it in this heat?"

She pushed her sombrero up and let it fall on her shoulders. Then she swept the light brown hair back from her face and smiled at him. "I'm fine."

"Sit in the shade of that ramada over there. He's gone to get us some food."

She walked over to the arbor to sit on a bench. Slocum and Chief watered the animals.

"Looks safe enough," Slocum said under his breath to the Apache.

Chief nodded his head. "We have a long ride to the next water."

"Figured we might go at night. If you don't mind."

Chief dismissed his concern with a head shake. "Be glad to get this over."

"So will I."

Two women in colorful skirts returned with the man in white clothing. They carried trays of food and set them on a table under the ramada.

"Eat *mi amigos*," the man announced while the two women chattered with Mary.

"Your man is an Apache?" he asked under his breath as Slocum filled his plate from the beans and fresh-cooked corn.

"Yes. Why?"

"I only wondered. We use to live in great fear of them."

"Chief might kill you, but he won't eat you."

The man swallowed hard and stepped along so Slocum was between him and the old Indian.

After they ate, they recinched their girths and left. Slocum turned back for one last look. He didn't trust the man who called himself the mayor. But he doubted the man could do much more than send word to El Maldito that they had been there. Probably hoping for some reward. Though Slocum had paid them for the food, the favor of a warlord like El Maldito was important to such men.

Another rest in late afternoon, and they rode under the stars that night. Chief found them a small spring at daybreak. They stopped there in the shade of a few mesquites and allowed their animals some rest.

"In four or five hour's ride tonight, we can make the hacienda of a friend," Slocum said. "We can really rest there. Senor Encoato will be a gracious host."

Mary smiled and nodded. "I'm sure ready to find a place to get some sleep."

By stars, they crossed the dry hills through steep canyon trails and went over a pass and down the far side into the desert again. The way was tough, but on the floor again they jogged their animals and Slocum was convinced by dawn they would be at his friend's hacienda gate.

Two men with rifles stopped them as the purple glow of dawn began to shine over the saw-toothed hills behind them.

"My name is Slocum. The patron knows me."

"Ah, *si*, senor, but we will accompany you to the hacienda. These are very bad times in our land and we can trust no one."

"I understand," Slocum said and they rode along through the irrigated dark vineyards and crops to the hulking hacienda looming ahead.

"Senor Slocum and his amigos are here," the man announced.

"Oh, he is an amigo of the patron," the voice from inside said and the gate was opened.

A white-bearded man rushed out to greet him. "The patron will be pleased you are here, senor."

"Don't wake him."

"Oh, he would be furious if we don't. Espinoza, go wake the patron. Tell him his amigo, Slocum, is here."

In a short while, the small figure of Richardo Encoato arrived in the courtyard. He rushed over to hug Slocum and bowed to Mary when he introduced her. "Welcome and who is this?"

"We call him Chief. He is a man who came to Mexico to help me."

"Ah, senor, you are most welcome to my hacienda and casa. Come with us. We will eat. I bet you are hungry. Where did you come from?"

"The Madres," Slocum said and began to explain his mission.

Richardo took Mary's arm and squeezed her hand as he nodded to Slocum's words, leading them into a grand dining room lighted with candles. The cool morning's air swept in the open French doors from the patio.

"Ah, this one called El Maldito is a bad hombre. Many in Mexico would reward you, too, if he was removed from power."

"Maybe if he was dead," Mary said. "His men murdered my husband across the border."

"This man is bad. Let us rise for a toast to his demise," Richardo said and stood up. "To his death!"

Even Chief joined in and pewter goblets clanked.

After the big breakfast of melons, tortillas, eggs and pork, Slocum took a bath and the maids helped him, giggling at the sight of him undressed as they dried him.

"What is wrong?" he asked with a towel around his waist as he waited for the return of his clothes, which were being laundered.

The full-faced one said. "Oh, you have such a *grande* sword."

The other more attractive one in her late teens grinned big at the discovery. "I have seen the stallion's and his is no larger."

"Maybe we can discuss this more later?" he asked with a wide smile.

They looked at one another and giggled. Then the fat one said, "Maybe tonight."

"Good. Tonight in my room." They smirked at him, agreed and then shook their heads in disbelief over the matter. They hurried for the door, wadding the used towels in their arms.

"Your clothes are being made ready," the fat one said to reassure him and closed the door after herself.

Dressed in freshly washed and ironed clothing, Slocum felt refreshed when he emerged an hour later. He found Richardo in the dining room.

"You have spoken of this bandit El Maldito." The man showed him to a chair and sat on the front edge of his own. "I have many guards out all the time against the likes of him and others. I have pleaded with the governor of Sonora for a company of *rurales* to be stationed out here. But he says I am too far out to do that.

"They rape my people, they rob the wagon trains I send to sell my produce and they rustle my cattle and horses."

"Is El Maldito the leader of all this?"

"He is but one of them. A man called the Scar is another. He is a mean *bastardo*, too."

"I can't rid the world of all the bad ones—"

"I know, Slocum. But if you find this one called Scar kill him, too."

"Where does he come from?"

"The dust of the desert—" Richardo shook his head so hard the black hair fell in his face. He swept it back with his palm. "Could I hire you to do that?"

"I'm not certain. I promised Duke Holden I would find the killers of the storekeeper in Bisbee. Then El Maldito killed my Apache scouts who were after the men who did the murder. Obviously their killers work for the chief outlaw."

"But you could get this one called Scar and I would pay you well."

"Maybe when I get back from Fronteras, I can help you."

"Hurry back then."

They drank the strong coffee the woman delivered. Both men stood when Mary entered the room. With her hair curled and done up, the beauty in her face radiated. She wore a colorful skirt and blouse.

"Ah, senora," Richardo said, took her hand, bowed, then he kissed her fingers.

Her face reddened at the attention and she thanked him, then took the chair he showed her.

"Such a lovely lady to ride across the hot desert. Would you stay with me as my special guest until Slocum can return from Fronteras?"

"I am afraid—"

He touched her lip with his finger. "No, you must say yes.

Your company makes this room glow and the desert will only steal the life from the petals of such a flower."

"I am flattered, but I am only a miner's widow—" She looked taken aback by his words.

"Such a man must have bragged every day that he had married royalty. You are so lovely."

She looked at Slocum for help.

"It's a fine offer, Mary, and he is a gentleman."

"But—"

"The road will be what he says, hot and dry. Beside Chief and I can do much more alone."

"So!" Richardo said, pointing at the high ceiling. "You will be my guest."

"I guess," she finally said.

"I will send along one of my best men, Benito, who knows the city well to assist you, Slocum. He also has informers there who can help you find these murderers."

"Good, that should help," Slocum looked across at Mary and nodded to reassure her.

She still looked taken aback by the man's request for her to remain there and the turn of events, but managed to say, "Yes, that might be very good."

"I'll get that killer," Slocum said to her. "You need not worry."

"Oh, I hope so."

Richardo put his hand on her forearm and leaned toward her, indicating Slocum. "I have known this man for long time. He is the best there is."

She agreed with short nods.

Later, Slocum met with Chief who was seated on a bench in the courtyard.

"In the morning we can head for Fronteras on fresh horses. His man Benito is going along to help us find this killer."

"Plenty good place to stay, too." The old man smiled and clapped him on the leg. "I see plenty good signs."

About then a buxom woman came from the back door of the kitchen with a tray for Chief.

Slocum excused himself, seeing the devil dancing in Chief's eyes at her approach.

"In the morning, we'll be saddled and ready by dawn."

Chief nodded he knew when and Slocum went back inside. In the hallway, he could hear Richardo explaining the paintings on the wall to Mary so he avoided them and slipped quietly down the hallway to his room.

A chance to rest some sounded good, so he toed off his boots and stretched out on top of the bed. The thick adobe walls held in the night's coolness and outside his French door the birds sang in the flower gardens.

The door creaked and he frowned as it came open. Slipping inside, the thicker-set maid held a finger to her mouth, then with a big grin closed the door, pushing the latch over to lock it.

"I saw you coming in for your siesta," she whispered.

He nodded sitting up and combing his hair back with his fingers.

"I wanted you before Silvia did."

"What is your name?"

"Lupe."

"Well, Lupe, gracias." He held out his arms.

She blinked her brown eyes as if shocked and helped him lift her blouse. When the garment was high over her head, he began to suckle on the large brown nipple and she moaned in pleasure.

Gunshots! Outside the hacienda, but he recognized them and moved her aside to get up and find his six-gun . . .

"I'll be back," he said to her and rushed out the door in his stocking feet.

"Raiders!" someone shouted.

More shots. What in the hell was happening? He burst in the dining room and met Richardo with his gun in hand running from the other end of the house.

"Front gate—" Richardo pointed his pistol in that direction and led the way.

More shots. Slocum was two feet behind the man when he jerked open the front door. Two men on horseback blazing away came under the arch. More shots from the guard on the wall.

Richardo took the one out on the left, Slocum the one on the right. He saw several of Richardo's men coming with pistols in their hands to join them.

The other raiders outside must have fled for the drum of retreating hooves was obvious as Slocum rushed to the gate in his stocking feet.

"Is anyone hurt?" Richardo asked aloud when they both stood under the arch and watched the bandits' dust.

"Morales is shot in the leg," the man on top said.

"Go get him down," he ordered. "Anyone else?"

"No, they rode up like some vaqueros riding through. When we did let two of them in the gate they began shooting."

"You did well," Richardo said to his men and turned to Slocum. "This won't be their last try either."

"You think these men work for Scar?"

"Bandits." Richardo shrugged. "Who knows. They were here to rob me."

"Are there any of the bandits still alive?"

"I will ask my foreman, Carlos."

"See that old Apache over there," Slocum said, motioning to the old man. "He can find out anything. Of course you might not want to know it all."

"Fine, we want to know."

"I'm going to find my boots," Slocum said. "These damn stickers are getting through into my socks and I need to pick them out."

"Later then," Richardo said, amused at his situation.

Slocum agreed, removing the socks full of goat heads and spines when he reached the tile of the porch. His soles felt like pincushions. He rubbed them off, but was certain he didn't have them all and gimped back down the hall to his room.

Certain he was alone, he looked up and down the hallway. No one in sight, he eased the door open and slipped inside. Sitting in the middle of the bed, naked as Eve, Lupe smiled big at him and held her globe-sized breasts up in each hand for him to see them.

"We don't have much time," he warned her.

"Get undressed then," she said, scooting her plump butt across the sheet to come off the high bed and join him.

Clothes flew and her full breasts dug into him as she fought off his shirt. In a minute, he was undressed and loading her in the bed. For a moment, he wondered about the open French doors, but decided the hell with it. He came up the valley between her sausage-shaped legs. A glance down at the dark patch of pubic hair, he grinned and hefted his half full rod up to enter her.

She raised herself up to meet him and moaned at his entry. His butt ached to pump it to her. She threw her head back in ecstacy at his first plunge. He was pounding her into the deep bed. His sword swelled large and larger. Her cunt responded and became tighter and tighter. Her pleas for more and more grew louder and she rocked on her back, making a large U shape with her body. Her legs wrapped around him as he drove faster and harder; then he felt relief coming up the seminal tubes like someone had squeezed his nuts—and he exploded inside her. She clung to him and strained, then after a long moment collapsed.

Her bleary brown eyes looked at him as she smiled. "Mother of God that was wonderful."

A quick kiss and he retreated. Whatever the bandit had to say he needed to hear. He quickly dressed and put on another pair of socks as she sat on the edge of the bed hugging her large breasts and smiling.

"What's so neat?" he asked sitting beside her and pulling on his boot.

"Oh, everything." And she threw her arms around him and drove her big boobs into him.

He kissed her and put on his other boot. Big bedful, but she was sweet.

11

"Who sent you?" Slocum demanded.

"No savvy?" The outlaw hung by his thumbs from the rafters. Stripped down to the bottom half of his underwear, the exposed wound in his side oozed blood. Slocum guessed he was about eighteen.

"Maybe you don't understand," the foreman Carlos said. "That Apache over there says for us to stick cactus spines in your balls."

"I don't care. Kill me."

"We won't kill you until you tell us who you work for. Spines in your balls, we don't care. But you won't die easy," the silver-haired forman said.

Barely able to touch the floor with his bare toes, the pain from his thumbs was causing him to sweat. Rivers ran down his snow-white chest and leather-brown face.

"I don't know—"

"Liar!"

"All right, I'll tell you if you cut me down."

"Who gave you the order to come here and try to rob us."

"Secatrese."

"Scar—" Richardo shook his head. "Why in the daylight?"

'Figured you'd be taking a siesta."

"Cut him down," Richardo ordered. "And shoot him outside

81

the wall. I want his head on a spike out at the main entrance to the ranch."

"His body?"

"Feed it to the hogs."

"But the padre—"

"This *bastardo* does not deserve any mercy. He would have shot you or raped your wife and children. No quarter for him."

"*Si*, patron."

Richardo motioned for Slocum to follow him and headed for the house. "I wish I could hire you to rid this land of that man and his bandits."

"It would not be easy."

"And I know"—he slammed his fist on the table—"there would be another bastard to take his place in six months."

Slocum agreed. The woman from the kitchen brought the whisky and glasses. Mary joined them, curious to know more about the shooting. Looking fearful, she shook her head at their words.

"Is there no end to these killers and thieves?" she asked.

Slocum saw a new light in her brown eyes and it was one of concern for his friend. The notion amused him a little, but he knew Richardo's wife had died two years before in childbirth. The man was handsome, though shorter even than she was. He had a nice appearance and looks. Besides he was rich, despite the inconvenience of the outlaws' siege of his hacienda. That, too, could be halted—but he wanted El Maldito first. Then he could talk business with his friend Richardo about the one called Scar.

"What can I do?" Richardo asked.

"Hire a spy to infiltrate them. Learn all you can. I'll get El Maldito, then I'll be back to help you."

"Yes, a spy. That would be a good idea. Why didn't I think of that before?"

"But he must be careful, whoever you send. The outlaw may have spies in your camp."

"Oh, I never thought of that." Richardo frowned at him.

"You'd better be on guard. He could be paying someone to give him information about the guards and setups here."

Richardo smiled at Mary who stood close by him. "Now even my family is suspect."

"Hey, you have lots of loyal people. But it only takes one," Slocum said. "I better accept your offer of fresh horses for Chief and me."

"I should go, too. I want those killers so bad," Mary said.

"Best you stay here. We'll be back in a short while.

"Besides you are like a bright lamp in this house. I would miss you," Richardo said and made her blush.

Slocum, the Apache and Richardo's man, Benito, left in late afternoon. They led a mule loaded with bedding and food. After parting with the sad-looking Mary, they short-loped their horses through the vineyards and fields of crops. The mule was well broke and kept pace in a swift trot. Beyond the hacienda's borders, they dropped to a jog in the blazing sundown that settled off in the west.

Slocum felt certain two day's hard ride and they'd be in Fronteras. Then they would need to locate the outlaw's lair. The Apache had little to say, but he never tired or complained either despite his age. Slocum wondered about that—was he sixty? Seventy or more? No telling, but he had seen much in his life.

Benito was a man in his thirties, extremely quiet, but quick to answer Slocum's questions. It was decided they would part before they reached the city. Slocum drew the man a map to where he planned to stay at Leona Sanchez's house.

"Many speak of Cochise as a great leader," Slocum said to Chief when they camped late in the night and sat at a small fire.

"He was a big man and spoke eloquently at meetings. He always led. He never sent anyone to do it. He always was a Chiricahua."

"What do you mean?' Slocum stirred the fire.

"He never trusted the other bands. He married a Warm Springs woman and they had an alliance. Victorio was his father-in-law and joined with the Apaches from Mexico, too. But Cochise considered the rest of the Apaches less than dirt."

"That why the Chiricahuas left San Carlos?"

Chief laughed and then shook his head in disgust. "Not only were they forced to live among their enemies, but they'd lost their lands. Their home. Cochise was dead by then, but moving them to San Carlos was bad for his people."

"What would they have done with all the silver in the Tombstone mines and copper in Bisbee if they'd kept the reservation that General Howard gave them?"

Chief shrugged as if he had no answer for him. "That was all inside their lands when Cochise made the treaty with him."

Slocum looked at the sky full of stars. Hundreds, maybe thousands of lives would have been saved. But destiny had another plan.

"You know General Howard had only one arm?" Chief said.

"You saw him?"

Chief nodded. "He spoke like a warrior. He had no fear in his eyes. He sat in council with Cochise and they talked on the far side of the Dragoon Mountains. That's where they made the treaty."

Slocum nodded. "Tom Jeffords was there?"

"Red Beard." Chief agreed by bobbing his head. "He was the agent. But they would not send him supplies because he was not one of them."

"One of them?"

In the dim light of the fire, the old man's sun-wrinkled face drew in a great grin. "He did not belong to the ring in Tucson."

Slocum agreed. He recalled that day in Mexico when he was working as a packer with Crook and, after much talking, Geronimo promised to surrender. Later that evening the civilian in charge of the army's beef contract gave the Chiricahuas whiskey and told them they'd hang in Arizona if they went back with Crook.

"Were you with them when Geronimo ran away after saying he would surrender to Crook?"

"Bad days for all Apaches," Chief said. "Whites, too."

"This man who had your grandson killed, El Maldito?" Slocum asked. "You know of him?"

Chief nodded. "I could have killed him once in the Madres. But I was lazy, knowing the men with him would make my escape hard if I exposed myself. So for that I have paid a big price."

Slocum nodded. It was why the old man was so set on this track-down. More even than the loss of the boy—he considered it his own fault.

"Tomorrow night we will be there. Leona Sanchez will put us up and help find him."

"Good," Chief said. "This is why I came when Mary said you would help me."

"I fear that my amigo Richardo is very taken by her."
Slocum shared a smile with Benito who sat to his right.

Chief bobbed his head across the fire from them. "She is a
very nice lady."

"Yes." Slocum agreed and listened to the coyotes yap.

"Speak my brothers. Tell us of the way and how," Chief said
and stood up to listen. Arms folded over his chest, the outline of
the coolie hat against the starlit sky, he nodded to his gods.
When they finally left, Chief sat down again.

"They have good news?" Slocum asked.

"Some, some not so good."

"Should we change our plans?"

The old man shook his head. When Slocum glanced at Benito, the man looked upset. But dismissed it with a shrug,

Fronteras bustled even after sundown with trade. Burro trains
filled the street and Slocum had to dodge them and the noisy
ungreased *carretas* that made great screaming noises as they
lumbered through the narrow streets. Past the square, he turned
off to the right in front of the great cathedral built by Father
Keno. It was one of many such churches the pioneer priest built
in a line of them that stretched clear to Tucson. Up the street
with the mule in tow, they arrived at a tall wooden gate. Slocum
dismounted to pull the bell rope.

"Who is there?"

"A friend of the senora's."

"What is your name?"

"Slocum."

"Oh, *si*, come in, senor."

Slocum nodded in approval to the Apache and they rode inside once the gate opened for them.

"Senor Slocum." The man bowed at the waist. "It has been a
while since you came to see us."

"I've been busy. This is Chief. Find him a room."

"I will, senor, and I will put up the horses—"

"Slocum!" Leona shouted from the second-story balcony in
a voice that rasped in a smoky way. "Why you old devil. Where
have you been? I thought you were dead."

Leona Sanchez charged down the stairs wrapping a robe
around her ripe form. "Who's your friend?"

"I call him Chief."

Her eyes narrowed and she looked hard in the light shafts that came though the trees at him. "Any friend of his I like."

Chief nodded and smiled. "He is a good one to ride with."

"Yeah, yeah—" The she broke down into laughter. Finally she managed to regain her composure. "Welcome to my casa. Juan can show you a place to stay, get you food—"

"I know. I be fine." Chief clapped her hand between his. "I be fine."

Slocùm nodded to him as she grasped his arm and drove him toward the house. "I got all choked up on the good man to ride with. Hell, I knew you were a good man to ride me." Her free laughter rolled out into the night.

She stopped inside the door, pressed her firm full breasts into him and threw her head back for him to kiss her. Their mouths met and he savored her hot tongue searching his mouth. The pressure of her ripe body against him.

At last, she buried her face in his vest. "Oh, I know only business ever brings you here. What do you need to find this time?"

"A killer named El Maldito."

She used a hand to sweep the hair from her face. Then she closed her eyes in disappointment. "He is very tough. Even the officials here fear him."

"His men killed a merchant in Bisbee. The mine wants him brought in or destroyed."

"You won't ever arrest him."

"You mean the authorities won't arrest him for me."

"No! They won't even dare arrest him for crimes he does in Sonora."

"Must be a tough hombre."

"He is the worst of the worst." She led him into the kitchen.

"Where does he live?"

"In the mountains west of here. It is a fortress. A cannon or two and some Gatling guns."

"How did he get so strong?"

"He has made lots of money, smuggling and robbing mine shipments." Then she turned to an older woman who appeared from the side room. "Fix him some food. He is famished." A smile on her face, the woman moved to stoke her large range with firewood.

Leona held up a bottle of wine and then as if satisfied, used the corkscrew to open it. Pouring the red wine in crystal goblets, she held one out to him.

"You are lucky. Maria has a fresh cut loin she bought today. Come and tell me all about where you have been for so long. I feared those brothers from Kansas had caught you."

"No, they've not been close lately."

"I wish you would stay here and forget this El Maldito." She motioned to the couch and sat down beside him covering her bare legs with the robe and smiling slyly at him.

"Maybe afterwards—"

"Oh, no, you will be off again and break my heart." She refilled his glass and put the bottle back on the table.

He reached over and squeezed her chin. "Ah, but our reunions are so wonderful."

She threw her blue eyes at the ceiling for celestial help.

12

"That's his fort." Slocum handed the Apache his field glasses for a view of the walled compound across the valley from them.

Chief's soft whistle indicated how impressed he was with the setup. Everything was cleared back for over a quarter of a mile. The cactus, boulders and even the greasewood was hacked off. Depressions had been filled in so there was no place to hide near the fort, only gritty bare ground graded up to the twelve-foot wall topped with corner towers that held Gatling guns. Definitely a military-designed fortress with a thick gate that was manned by a half dozen guards on the ground. They took nothing for granted, stopping all who wished to enter and searching them for weapons. The line of those waiting to enter was long. Burro trains bringing firewood, water and supplies were closely observed and inspected. Several women carrying wares were physically handled by the security men to be certain they had no weapons under their clothing.

No wonder the law never bothered him. It would require open warfare to take Maldito on—artillery and an army. Then there was no sign they'd be successful short of a long siege.

Who was this El Maldito anyway?

"Look." Chief pointed to the train of mules coming from the north.

"The smugglers. Those could be the ones that killed the merchant in Bisbee and the Apaches."

Slocum took the glasses and viewed the lead rider. A swarthy, black-bearded man with broad shoulders. Bandoliers crisscrossed his chest and he wore a red sash around his waist. Dust floured and slant-eyed for the sun's glare, he looked the role of a ruthless outlaw. His heavily armed men driving the mules looked equally as tough. A half dozen of the border's toughest bandits all headed for the headquarters of the terror of Sonora—El Maldito City.

"Those are the killers?" Chief asked. His eyelids drew close and the glare in them looked deadly.

"Yes."

"We must wait and see when they leave. Away from the fort we can pick them off one at a time."

"It will be the only way," Slocum agreed.

"I will stay here and watch for them to leave again," Chief said.

"Be careful. Better draw back or they will eventually spot you."

The old man nodded.

"I have some jerky and I'll leave my water."

"Good. When they start out again, I will come to her place and find you."

"Remember they've killed some good men."

"I know. Take my horse. They could find him."

"How will you—"

"I am old, but not that old." He laughed and smiled big at Slocum. "I can still steal a horse, too. I have not forgotten the old ways."

Slocum rode back to Fronteras by another route than the one they had taken there. He arrived in late afternoon at Leona's gate. Leona's top hand, Juan, quickly opened it and Slocum rode in; she came running to greet him.

"At last you are back. I have guests coming for supper. They may be able to help you."

"Who?" He dropped heavily from the saddle.

"Colonel Milano and his aide Lieutenant Valdez."

"Oh."

"They are very trustworthy. They can tell you all about this bandit."

"The fewer people who know why I am here, the safer we'll be. Including you."

She hugged his arm. "These are good men. I know them well, trust me."

"This man is a deadly killer and he must know by now my purpose. He would kill a dozen men like they were lice if he thought they were in his way."

"Where is the old man?" She looked around.

"Scouting El Maldito's operation."

"I wondered. Take a bath. I have some new clothes laid out for you and then we will have supper with these men."

"They know who I am?"

"No. But they can help you. They hate this El Maldito. They know what he does and are powerless to do anything about him."

"Why?"

"I will let them explain."

He looked back to the courtyard. Juan had led the horses off to the stable. Slocum trusted no one in Fronteras, but her and the old Apache. Anyone else in this deal was suspect. Except perhaps Benito and Slocum had no idea where he might be at the moment. All he could do was hope that she had not turned his hand by inviting these army men. El Maldito must be paying lots of spies and informers for any information that was a threat to him. That was how he held such an evil empire intact—knowing what his enemies planned and smashing them short of any surprise.

"Come, we have lots of hot water." She pulled him by the arm to the room downstairs where the copper tub sat.

After his bath, he put on the clothes Leona had gotten for him: a blowzy white cotton shirt and and striped brown pants; a tan silk sash for the waist in place, he looked at the new boots made of soft calfskin leather. He examined the workmanship turning one over in his hand. The new leather smell curled up his nose.

"Like them?" she asked from the doorway.

"You spoil me. Yes, they are very nice. But the size?"

"I made a pattern from your old ones while you bathed yesterday."

"But in one day, he made these boots?"

She shrugged and pursed her lips as if it were nothing. "Money can speed things."

Seated on the bed, he chuckled pulling on his new footgear. "Your generosity overwhelms me."

"I could do better than that if you stayed in my bed more often."

He looked at the pointed toes and shook his head. "I would only bring you grief."

"I'm grateful for when you come by. Come downstairs and we will have a glass of wine."

He stood up and stomped lightly in his new boots; they felt like gloves. "Wonderful, my dear. I'm coming."

"What did you find out there?"

"A fortress. Obviously he would not be taken lightly. Short of an army and lots of artillery, his place is impenetrable."

"Milano will no doubt want your opinion of that situation tonight."

"He wants to take the place?"

"I think Mexico City feels El Maldito is getting too powerful, that he may try to take over Sonora." She went behind the bar and uncorked a bottle, pouring him a crystal glass full of red wine. "So you may have allies in this business."

"He'd better be ready to move swiftly. El Maldito will know his plans in no time."

"It's one of many things that the colonel is concerned about. He even fears that El Maldito has offered some of his own officers roles if they revolt."

"Money sure talks and obviously he has been busy acquiring it through his smuggling and other illegal operations."

"Colonel Milano is a stiff shirt, but he listens, too."

Aromas from Maria's kitchen filled the house with the fragrance of roasted beef and cooked vegetables. Fresh and clean, Slocum lounged on the couch and toasted Leona's beauty and health. She sat opposite him on the stuffed sofa. The deep cleavage set apart her pear-shaped breasts as she exposed her shapely calves for him to view on the sofa between them. Enough woman there, he could have skipped the meeting and meal with Milano. Instead, he would have hauled her fine, hard ass upstairs to the deep feather bed and screwed her till sundown. But the rock hard erection in his new pants could wait, too.

"Colonel Emanuel Milano," she said, introducing the man with the bill cap under his arm and a white dress uniform. He snapped to attention.

"Senor, welcome to Mexico. My aide, Lieutenant Benito Valdez."

"Nice to meet you, Colonel and you, too, Lieutenant." He shook their hands and she showed them to the living room. Milano was small man, straight shouldered with a trimmed mustache, perhaps in his early forties. His aide was hardly out of his teens, a weak-chinned young man who looked ready to slump at any moment, but military training had taught him better. Taller than his boss, he was thin and the dress uniform fit him less well.

She showed them to the sofas and sat down next to Slocum at a respectable distance.

"The senora said you are looking for killers," Milano said.

"They robbed a storekeeper in Bisbee and stole his money and supplies."

"Ah, you know these men's names?"

Slocum shook his head. "They work for El Maldito."

"You have proof?"

"His mule train that smuggles in mescal and other liquor was the one involved in the murder."

"But no names?"

"No names."

"How could you expect to find them if you have no names?"

"I already have some of the killers in custody in Bisbee. No doubt, after their interrogation, the law there now knows the other names and will wire me a list, I am certain, of the guilty when I get in touch."

"Let us send that wire in the morning. I need a reason to take on this bandit." Milano held up his index finger. "One name is enough. People fear him so much they won't report any crimes he commits, because he kills all the witnesses. He does not scare you, senor?"

"No. His men killed two good scouts of mine on this side of the border."

"Ah! Murder in Mexico. Who were these men?"

"Apache scouts I hired to trail the train. But I have no bodies. They ambushed me and I couldn't locate the corpses."

"They were killed?"

"Oh, yes, in a vision, a *bruja* saw them lying facedown in a dry wash, shot in the head."

Milano smiled. "What else did she see?"

"Trouble for me."

"Trouble for everyone. Maldito extracts much money from merchants and businessmen and they pay him and never will testify against him," the lieutenant said.

"Mexico City thinks he is trying to take control of Sonora and maybe other states on the frontier."

Slocum tented his fingertips and tapped his nose. "But the minute you make plans to take his fortress he will know and be prepared."

"What do you say to do?" Milano asked.

"Take two cannons out with little guard as an exercise, divert it to the hill over the fort and blast off the two towers with Gatling guns. They will never raise the cannons high enough to shoot at your guns. You can pick them off one by one and then attack the gate."

"Sounds too easy. You must have seen this fort, senor." His thin eyebrows arched in a frown. The colonel looked hard at him for the answer.

"His guns are all aimed for a frontal attack."

"Maybe you need a commission in the *federales*."

"No. I want the killers."

Milano nodded. "You know I have had spies look at that place and they say we could never take it. But they were not soldiers, were they?"

"Yes, they probably were and saw that bare ground with no place to hide when soldiers advanced and those Gatling guns spraying death and cannon fire."

"But you can see the Achilles heel, no?"

"Yes. Tomorrow, I will get the list of those other killers from Marshal Madden in Bisbee or Holden at the mine."

"Fine, senor. That would justify my actions."

"We'd better eat or the food will be cold," Leona said and herded them to the dining room.

After the two men left later that evening, Leona poured the two of them glasses of wine and they sat on the sofa, sipping it. "Well, he is all business, isn't he?"

"I like him. He talks straight. I trust my first impressions. I'd ride with him."

Leona scooted close and on her knees, she clinked glasses with him. "Now I have done all your business—rape me."

"Here?"

"Yes," she said and pushed her breasts at him.

"You mean tear off your clothes and take you?"

"Yes." A warm smile crossed her face. "I want to be ripped apart."

"But your clothes cost many pesos—"

"To hell with what they cost. I want you to ravage me."

He leaned forward and put both their glasses down. Then, when he straightened, his eyes narrowed. "You may not like it."

"You can't do anything to me I won't like."

He reached over and grasped the dress in both hands and tore it open. Out spilled her solid breasts and he fondled them with both hands until she was as tall as she could get on her knees. Then he shoved her down on the couch, jerked open his pants and his ripe hard-on unfolded like a great probe. He shoved up wads of skirt and slips, roughly parted her legs, and climbed on top of her.

"Yes, yes, rape me," she whispered in anticipation. "Oh, my God, you are—"

Without any care, he rammed it home. The wet gates parted and soon he was grasping both cheeks of her hard ass and shoveling the coal to her. Their pubic bones ground hard against each other. When he looked down her head was thrown back and the cords of her throat were exposed as she moaned in pleasure. It only fueled him to pump her harder. The hard stick of her clit gouged the upper surface of his swollen dick.

The walls of her cunt tightened and she went limp for a short while, emerging bleary-eyed. A smile on his lips over her shattered condition, he raised up. His dick was painfully swollen, and he ripped off her dress. His victim was now stark naked. He pushed her facedown on the sofa, then raised her onto her knees. He spread the cheeks of her butt apart and started the nose of his dick into her ass.

"Oh," she moaned as he forced himself inside her. The head of his pecker was soon inside the tight passage. She began to pound the couch with her fists as he sought deeper and deeper penetration, holding her by the waist as he stood behind her. Then three fourths of the way in her, he knew the explosion was coming. He fought harder and deeper. The tingling in his balls told him enough. Hard pressed to her half moons, he pulled her tight against his belly and he came. The blast was hard and he felt the fire of it exploding inside her.

She fainted.

Seated on the floor and dizzy-headed, he looked over at his victim as she lay on the sofa. Their glances met. She formed a weak smile.

"By God, that was a real rape." She reached out and feebly patted him. "Oh hell, I loved it."

Slocum's mind wasn't on raping her any longer. It was on all that he needed to accomplish. Telegraph Bisbee. Meet with Colonel Milano. Attack the fort and get the hell out of Mexico. No, he still had his friend Richardo and Mary to help . . . but one thing at a time.

He swept Leona up in his arms and carried her into the bedroom. In a one-handed sweep he ripped back the covers and then deposited her on the feather bed.

She held out her arms to him. He nodded and toed off his new boots.

13

Next morning in the telegraph office, Slocum had a crawly feeling—something was wrong. He wore the six-gun and it was handy but he was not in a den of friendly or even neutral people. He could tell the situation was amiss after he paid for the telegram to Duke Holden, Mine Offices, Bisbee, Territory of Arizona, U.S.A. Something in his way the operator frowned and took his two pesos for the wire. His attitude made Slocum aware he might feel threatened.

What were the names of the other men in the killing that got away? Simple enough, but no doubt in his mind, El Maldito would know about the message shortly. After Slocum left the office, he slipped in the alley beside the adobe building and waited. In minutes, a boy burned out of the office and came by his position in the alley. He shot out a hand, caught a sleeve and he dragged the sputtering youth into the shadows.

"What do you want me for?" the boy of perhaps fifteen babbled.

"Where in the hell are you headed in such a damn hurry?"

"I-I must—"

"Tell El Maldito something?" He jerked him close to his face.

"No-no, senor."

"Then where were you going?"

"To see my *madre*."

96

Slocum whipped out his knife and laid the blade to the side of the youth's neck. "You want to ever eat again, you'd better tell me where you really were going."

"To tell Senor Marcos—"

"That I sent a telegram to learn the men's names."

"*Si.*"

Slocum wearied of the boy's slow answers. "Where's this Marcos at?"

"The cantina."

"Hell, there's hundreds of them in this town. Which one?" His impatience was about to boil over with this one. All the time, he kept an eye out for anyone coming out of the telegraph office or anyone who might notice them.

"La Paloma."

"Where?"

"On Verde Street."

Slocum tightened his grip on him. "You know how to get out of town?"

"*Si*, senor."

"I see you in town again, I'll cut your bag off. You go back and tell them anything, I'll feed you to the buzzards. You savvy?"

"Oh *si*, Mother of God I understand." Trembling in his hold, the boy held his hands together. "No one . . . I tell no one, senor. Oh, please, spare me."

"Promise me you'll get the hell out of the city."

"I swear on my mother's grave, senor."

"Get the hell out of here." He gave him a shove and a kick in the seat of his pants.

The boy tore off down the alley. Slocum watched him run away and then he put away his knife in the sheath behind his back. He needed to meet this Marcos on Verde Street at the La Paloma Cantina. Perhaps the colonel did, too. No doubt he was a link to the bandit El Maldito. Also, the operator of the telegraph office was involved. The colonel had some problems to solve, but once the commander knew some answers, the retribution would be swift.

The real thing vexing to Slocum was how they would handle the return telegram. They might keep the answer. Either way, he didn't trust the man working in the telegraph office. But short of going to the colonel for help, he'd have to wait and see.

Keeping an eye out, he dodged through neighborhoods, yards and around hanging wash to see if they had put someone out to follow him. He stood back in the shadows and waited, but no one came; satisfied, he went on to Leona's place.

"Where have you been, my lover?" she asked, meeting him at the open doorway when he crossed the patio.

"Oh, finding who I can trust and can't." Then he hugged and kissed her. "We'd better send word to the colonel. We already have some problems he needs to know about."

"Juan can take him a message."

"I'll write him a note. Then I need to go and check on the old man out at the fort."

"Your Apache?"

"Yes."

"Oh. He's asleep in the guest room over the stables. Came in right after you left. Ate some of Maria's food and said he had not slept in a long time. Juan took him down there."

"Good. He say anything about the fort?"

She shook her head. "What was he looking for?"

"A way to get inside."

"He said it was a very tight place."

"That means an Apache can't squeak inside."

She laughed. "Write what the colonel needs to know. Then you can take a siesta."

"Sounds wonderful," he said, sitting down at her desk and dipping the straight pen in the inkwell.

Colonel,

The operator at the telegram office acted suspicious at my wire to Bisbee. He sent a boy I intercepted to tell a Marcos at the La Paloma Cantina on Verde Street about my wire. Let me know your plans,

Slocum

He blew the ink dry and folded it.

Leona called out, "Juan, Senor Slocum has a letter for you to take to the colonel." The man swept off his sombrero and came in the room.

"Here is the note." Slocum handed it to Juan. "He may have a reply."

"I will take it to him, right now."

"*Gracias*," Slocum said and the man hurried off. He turned to Leona. "I am concerned they may threaten you over my presence here."

"I would risk it."

"These are not nice men."

"They know I have friends in high places that would scorch the earth to find them if they harmed me."

"That might not be good enough. These are really tough hombres."

"Oh, let me worry about that—"

He kissed her hard on the mouth. "I want nothing to happen to you. Keep the gates closed and be very careful."

Bent half backwards in his arms, she put the back of her hand to her forehead. "Whew, what about you? You turn me afire."

"Think how fine that will be after dark." He stood her up and pecked her forehead.

"After dark?" she whined.

He slapped her with the palm of his hand on her fanny. She scooted forward and then laughed. "Take a siesta. Supper will be ready at six."

He found the shaded hammock on the patio in back of the two-story house and toed off his boots, hung his gun belt on a straight-back chair and sunk into the comfort of the suspension. In minutes, his heavy eyelids closed and he was asleep.

A sharp sound awoke him. Still numb, he listened and half sat up. Leona was arguing fiercely with someone on the other side of the house. Gun in his hand, he hit the tile in his stocking feet. He crossed the flower-strewn patio to the side of the building. From that point he could count five men in the courtyard. Damn. What he'd worried about the most had happened: El Maldito's men had found him and she wouldn't tell them where he was.

Then an arrow split the air and thudded hard into a human body. It was a sound he could never forget from his days as a army scout. The outlaws shouted, gunshots were fired. Slocum stepped around the corner. His gun cocked, he cut down two of the bandits. The others were on the run for the gate. More arrows flew into them, two of them fell down screaming. Hard hit by a feathered projectile.

Leona raced out of the gun smoke. One outlaw made it to his horse. He gave Slocum a clear shot when he sat upright in the saddle. Hit hard, the bandit cartwheeled off the far side.

Slocum gathered her in his left arm, holding two shots for any survivors. She trembled in his grasp. Then he saw the old man in his breechcloth and knee-high boots standing on the tile roof of the stables. Slocum nodded in approval to the Apache armed with his bow and arrows.

"You all right?" Slocum asked her.

"Sure, sure, I'll be all right." She rubbed her arms as if to awaken them. "They were tough like you said."

"How many got away?" the Apache asked, already down on the ground by rappelling a tree.

"I'm not certain that any did. The police will be here in minutes—" Slocum wondered what he should do about them.

"You know the police?" he asked her.

A smug smile swept her face. "You let me handle them."

They didn't have to wait long for them to arrive. Two policemen in tan uniforms came rushing through the gate. They looked about at the carnage and the older one drew back his shoulders. "What happened here, senor?"

"Oh, Captain," Leona said in her sweetest voice and stepped forward. "These banditos were trying to rob me and these two nice men stopped them."

"Captain," the young officer said. "Some have been shot by arrows." The policeman's eye were big as saucers over his discovery.

"My Apache friend doesn't like bullets. They hurt his ears."

"Oh," the captain said and made a note on a small pad from his pocket with a pencil. "Are they all dead?"

Slocum shook his head. "But they will be in a short while."

"No need to find a doctor?"

"That's up to you."

The man nodded. "My name is Fredrick Mendoza."

"They call me Slocum, Captain, and his Apache name is hard to pronounce, so we call him Chief."

"Good idea. That is Phillipe, my patrolman. It is his first case of so much death."

"I understand."

"Captain Mendoza, perhaps we should have a drink and discuss this further in my casa," Leona said, taking his arm.

"Phillipe, throw them in the *carreta* and take them all down to the jail. We can decide about who needs care later."

"*Si, mon Capitán*, but I have no *carreta*."

Mendoza made an impatient face at his man. "Go out in the street and find one. Tell them this is police business and we need them to help us."

"*Si, capitán*." the patrolman saluted and rushed off.

Chief made sure none of them had any weapons and he squatted down to watch them. He motioned with a head toss for Slocum to go inside with them. That he could handle them as the wounded began to moan and cry.

Slocum knew they'd get no sympathy from the old man, though he would have liked to interrogate a couple of them. He watched Leona smother the policeman with her charm and sweetness. Then he heard more horses coming up the street; both he and Mendoza rushed out outside to see the source.

Lieutenant Benito Valdez and a small company of soldiers had arrived. The junior officer frowned at the men lying about. "I got here too late?"

"For the fun, yes," Slocum said. "They must be his men, too."

"I have the telegraph operator and his associates arrested," Valdez said and dismounted.

"Ah, maybe you wish to have these hombres, too?" Mendoza asked as if he didn't want to mess with them.

"Captain—"

"My man Phillipe has commandeered a *carreta*," Mendoza said and extended his hand toward the the gate and the little man in white cotton clothes standing beside his burros.

"Load them up," Valdez ordered and his men obeyed. Then he turned and thanked the policeman and his assistant. "Senor Slocum, the colonel requests you come by the headquarters, sir."

"My pleasure. Tell him I will be there within the hour."

"Very good. Senora, I hope you have no more bad experiences," Valdez said and bowed to her.

"Oh, Lieutenant," she said, "with such able men as you all I am sure they won't try anything again."

Slocum hoped not. He headed for the stables. Strange that Benito had not checked back with him. Perhaps he should check on him, too. But what worried him more was how they had only scratched the surface of El Maldito's army. Infesting the telegraph office and much more—maybe Milano should worry about his own ranks of men for traitors.

He brought his horse out and saddled him just as the army was preparing to leave with the *carreta* full of dead and dying outlaws. The ungreased axles screamed and the man had to whip his burros to get them to pull the load. Captain Mendoza had kissed Leona's hand, then gave a salute to Slocum before heading out the gate after the cart.

Slocum winked at his Apache squatted in the shade. "We are rid of some more."

The somber note almost masked the slight smile. "Many more."

"Yes, I think so, too. Many more."

"Oh, you two are my heroes. You must eat something before you ride out to the headquarters," she insisted.

"Chief can eat something. I'll eat when I get back."

She shook her head in disapproval, then she came over, stood on her toes and kissed him. "Be careful."

"Always." He mounted, shared a reassuring nod with his man and rode out the gate. Maybe Milano had a plan. He was ready to have all this over.

He threaded the traffic of street vendors, pack burros, even goats and soon was at the army's headquarters. Sentries stood rifle ready at the front entrance.

Slocum dismounted and spoke to the one in charge. "My name is Slocum. I am here to see the colonel."

The man saluted him. "Private, take this man's horse. Come this way, senor, the colonel is expecting you."

"My lady friend's man Juan came here this morning with a message for the colonel. I have not seen him since."

"Oh, he left here hours ago."

"Gracias," Slocum said, wondering where Juan went as he followed the man down the hallway. Two more armed guards stood at the entrance of the commander's office. Then they went

inside where a young man who must have been the colonel's secretary greeted them.

"Senor, the colonel awaits you." He opened the door and announced Slocum's arrival.

"So kind of you to come," Milano said, extending his hand.

After Milano showed him to a chair, Slocum told him about the attempt to get him at Leona's house and the rest.

"I think there is only one thing to do. Storm that fort."

"It will have to be done with care and enough artillery to blast the towers and the gate. My Apache says you can't get in there by scaling the walls or slipping inside."

"He should know. We know now what Maldito's ambitions are from what those telegraph spies told us a little while ago. Thanks to your help. He intends to control the northern half of Mexico."

"How many of his men are in your army?"

"You mean men who would join him?"

Slocum nodded and tented his fingers. "I am concerned he is deeper rooted than we know."

"You think I will have a revolt of my men if I attack him?"

Slocum touched the end of his nose with his fingertips. "I'm not certain, but if he has men running the telegraph, why not in your ranks as well?"

"Damn, you worry me."

"Better to worry now than have them desert to the enemy under fire."

Milano closed his eyes and nodded. "In two days, we will strike his fort at dawn. Using your plans of attack."

"It should go well."

"Will you join me?"

"Of course."

After he left the headquarters, he rode back swiftly to Leona's place. Filled with a million questions in his mind about what might happen next, he rang the bell. Chief came and opened the gate.

Slocum searched around. "Where's Juan?

The Apache shrugged. "She wondered, too."

"Those damn bandits must have him—somewhere."

Chief nodded.

He agreed. "Now, I'll need to find some guards for here."

"I can find some; you have enough worries," she said.

Where was her man Juan? Lots of unanswered questions. He put an arm around Leona's shoulder and guided her toward the casa. He'd better go to figuring it out some. That might start with Marcos at La Paloma Cantina.

14

It was past midnight. Slocum stood in the shadows off Verde Street watching the comings and goings at the La Paloma Cantina. He eased across the dirt street and into the alley filled with stinking garbage. A stud cat was making bull-like yowls somewhere off in the darkness. No doubt after some pussy in heat from the sounds of his commanding voice. Then a back door opened a crack letting a sliver of yellow light fall on the heaps of trash.

Slocum heard sharp voices. Angry ones, and he moved closer to hear the words. Arguing in earnest. That was when the tail of a cat came into the light. It was like a stiff wind, first making small waves then going straight at attention. The tail remained just so, even when the twice as large male leaped out of the darkness, pouncing on her like a hawk taking a mouse. She gave a cry of pain as he stuffed his organ to her in a powerful lurch of his hind feet.

His teeth sunk into her neck to hold her. She fought to escape. The shrill protest of her cries to his intrusion grew louder. The tomcat's muscles strained as he plunged deeper and deeper into her with each stroke. Then he threw back his head, roared like a lion and with one great final leap came inside her. His effort shot them out of the light zone.

Unfortunately for the tomcat, his super erection and the contractions of his mate's cunt had bound them together. The frenzied female charged into the darkness with her protesting connected rider being hauled along after her; his screams mixed with hers, they made an unholy chorus amidst the rattle of trash and old bottles clinking.

Voices came from inside the cantina. "It's only some cats screwing in the alley—"

"You be sure," someone ordered.

Slocum eased himself behind some barrels. He removed his hat to cut his outline and could see the big burly figure stalking around the room through the half-opened doors. The size and mannerisms of the man made him think that he was looking at El Maldito.

Hand on the butt of his six-gun, Slocum considered his next move. He could do folks a big favor if that was the man. But how could he be certain? Where were their horses? Only a few mules and burros at the hitch rack in front—nothing to ride in this alley.

If it was El Maldito in that room, how many more were in there with him? It could be like swatting at a hornet and unleashing a whole nest of them. Better yet, despite the word he sent by Juan to the colonel, it seemed that no one had checked on this cantina. Slocum shook his head and crouched down uncomfortably behind some barrels. He could hear bits of the conversation from the back room—who was the defector? Juan or the colonel?

If it was Juan, he needed to get back to Leona's place. She was in jeopardy. They could over run the Chief and—damn: What did he need to do next? Was that bearded bastard El Maldito or not?

Better find out. He drew his Colt and stepped out from behind the barrels. He looked both ways and saw nothing. Ten steps over the debris and he was at the back door. One shot in that small room would snuff out the lights. His first one had to count.

A few feet from the door, the arguing grew louder again.

"—who is he?"

"Some gringo bounty hunter."

"Why can't you kill him?"

Slocum used his foot to kick open the door and, gun first, he charged in. "Get your hands up."

"What the hell—" The black-bearded one went for his own gun.

Two, maybe three others in the room. Slocum's Colt blasted and the lights went out. Orange gunshots blazed in the room's darkness and the cloud of eye-stinging black powder caused them all to cough. Closest to the back door, Slocum eased out.

He busted the next bandit over the head when he came out coughing up his guts. The second escapee caught the same treatment in his moment of helplessness and after being hit over the head, he, too, spilled facedown on the garbage. Where was El Maldito? Had he wounded him? Like a half-dead rattlesnake, he might only be waiting on his chance to strike again.

Slocum's ear was turned toward the dark door. The acrid-smelling pistol was close by his face. He listened intently. He thought he could hear someone dragging themselves across the floor, but couldn't place where they were from his position beside the door. He dried his left hand on his new pants.

How long should he wait? Patience had to be on his side. Little doubt the other man was hit.

"What's going on, boss?" Voices broke in the room.

"The bastard is out there. Don't light no damn lights. Go get him."

Slocum retreated enough to cover the doorway. He had three shots left and no time to reload. He reached down, drew the .30 caliber Colt he kept in his boot and stuck it in his waistband; that gave him eight shots.

A figure loomed in the doorway and Slocum cut him down before he could even get his pistol up. A second one blasted away, emptying his revolver while he was still inside. His bullets filled the air with adobe dust as they hit the wall opposite the door. It also made everyone in the room cough on all the gun smoke. That led to more cursing and angry voices.

Slocum used a barrel for cover and fired another round into the doorway. It turned out lucky, for another bandit shouted, "I'm hit."

"Let's get the hell out of here—before he kills all of us."

"Yeah, what's he got out front?"

"Clear the damn way!" a familiar-sounding voice commanded.

In the stinking garbage pile, Slocum's back against the wall, he realized he may have wounded the big man, but he was far from dead. Might be time for him to relocate.

15

"You are certain that you shot El Maldito?" Leona asked as she helped undress him, wrinkling her nose at the smell of his clothing. "Whew."

"Positive. I hit him, but he was still giving orders when they took him out. Must have rode his own horse as far as I could tell, but they filled the street with lots of bullets when they made a break for it."

"You shouldn't have taken them on alone."

"I know, but I wanted him stopped. Say, did Juan come home yet?"

"No and I am worried about him."

He tested the steaming water in the tub. Sure hot enough. Richardo's man Benito hadn't shown up either. All very strange. *Whew*. The water was hot when he slipped down into the tub.

"When does the colonel need you?" she asked, using a soft brush and soap on his back.

"In the morning."

She nodded and used the brush on his back. The action felt good on his tight muscles.

"Are his clothes ready to wash?" Maria asked from the doorway.

"Yes, come get them. He's in the tub. They smell bad."

"Yes, they do," the housekeeper said, snatching them up. "You sleep in the garbage pile?"

"Not this time." He laughed at her accusation. "I was sober, too."

"Has Juan came back yet?" Leona asked her.

"No, and I am worried. He always comes right back from the things you send him on."

"He wasn't in that cantina," Slocum said. "And I didn't find him in the garbage out in back."

Maria stopped in the doorway, shaking his clothes at him. "I can tell from these that you looked all over, too."

Left alone with Leona, he wondered if the man went home. "He have a wife and family?"

"Juan? Oh, no. His people live down by Vera Cruz. He has no one here."

"No girlfriend?"

"Not one that he ever told me about."

"I don't like him not coming back. But like Benito, I don't know where to start looking for him either."

"Slocum!" Chief hissed from the front room for him.

"What?" He stood up, water cascading off of him, and grabbed a towel to tie around his waist.

"Someone outside is trying to get in."

"At the gate?"

"No, they tried the back gate but it was locked."

Slocum took his six-gun out of the holster.

"You can't go like that," Leona protested. She swept up some clean pants and pursued him. "These should fit you."

On the patio, he waved her back. Chief set out for the stairs that would take him to the second floor over the stables and give him a view of the ground beyond the high wall. Slocum decided to follow him. Nothing looked threatening in the yard.

When they reached the second story, Slocum moved on the Apache's heels. A window sprang open and Slocum peered down at the dark ground. Then he spotted a figure wearing a hat.

"Get your hands in the air!"

A shot answered him. Slocum replied with his own gun, then ducked back. Nothing. He nodded to the Chief in the half-light of the upstairs.

"I may have hit him."

"I go see."

"Be careful. He might be playacting."

The bowlegged Apache rumbled back down the flight. Slocum almost laughed—even bowlegged he could outrun a young man. Carefully he looked again out in the starlight and tried to see any sign of the figure he'd shot. But nothing moved. He hurried down the stairs and finally took the pants from Leona.

"You'd better go put on your socks and boots," she said.

"I know, stickers and thorns."

He looked after Chief and then decided to run in the house for his footgear. He had the second boot on when she shouted, "He has someone."

"Coming," he said and rushed out, pulling the second boot on and stomping it on his foot.

"Who is it?"

Leona shook her head when he went past her.

He could see the man's bloody shirt and him holding his arm. "Who're you?"

The hard-faced individual stuck out his chiseled jaw and never blinked. His attitude threw Slocum into gear. Grabbing the man's shirt with his fist, Slocum jerked the man close and slapped him hard. "Wake up and speak to me."

"Watrous." The man gave his name.

Getting a better grip of the shirt, Slocum spoke in his face. "Who do you work for?"

"El—El Maldito."

"Where is her man, Juan?"

"At the fortress."

"Would Maldito exchange your ass for his?"

The man shook his head. He didn't know.

"A man called Benito?"

The man made a *no comprende* look. That didn't surprise Slocum. Benito might not be using his real name. "How many men are in his jail?"

"A dozen."

"Why are you here?"

"I was only checking to see if you were here."

"What then?"

Watrous shrugged again.

"Get to talking." He shook him good to get his attention. "What would they do if I was here?"

"Kill you."

Leona inhaled deeply at the words. Chief nodded and his eyes glinted like hard diamonds in the half-light. Slocum nodded; there was still lots he didn't know. Maybe in the raid on the fort they would get the one in charge—daylight should tell him more.

16

Slocum sat his horse beside the colonel's fancy bay. The jingle of
artillery setting up sounded loud, but definitely muted all it could
be. Both pieces of Milano's artillery were being placed on the
rise in the purple predawn. Cannoneers were busy loading and the
officer in charge was making calculations for the first shots. The
gun crews, ready to fire, stood at attention awaiting the command.

"Fire until the mission is complete," Milano ordered.

Slocum tried to close off his ears even at his distance from
the guns—he knew the percussion would hurt them. He handed
the glasses to Chief when the first muzzle roared sending a
charge screaming into the predawn quiet. The brilliant explosion on the wall drew Slocum's nod. The left-hand turret was
destroyed. One deadly rapid-fire Gatling gun was gone. Round
two struck the wall ten feet left and the gunnery officer immediately gave the new coordinates to gun number one.

The uproar from inside the fortress was loud. Men giving
orders. The next round from the Colonel's artillery only gave
the gate a glancing blow. But when cannon number two fired,
the second tower disappeared. Number one's next round
struck the gate again, this time splintering it open in a smoky
blast.

A cannon on the wall south of the gate answered. But the
grenade blew up far underneath the hilltop position. The second
gun answered it and that section of the wall was soon notched

113

away. Through the smoke and dust, Slocum felt sure the gun had been destroyed or blown off the ledge.

"Get the cannon on the right," Milano shouted.

It thundered a round at the hillside below them. Both answered it. The result was a tremendous explosion that threw bodies in the air.

"Bugler, sound the charge!" the colonel ordered.

At the first sound of the brass horn, a scream came like a wave and the thunder of horses and charging foot soldiers filled the air until they dissolved the bugler's attempt to rally them.

There were a few feeble gunshots from the top of the wall and the first wave of *federales* stormed the gate. Fighting grew more intense from the sounds of the shots. Slocum nodded to the colonel. "Chief and I want to find him."

"Be careful, *mi amigo*. If I ever need a military strategist, I want to call on you. Obviously you have done this before."

"A few times."

"*Vaya con Dios,*" the officer said after them.

Slocum and Chief bailed their horse off the steep slope. Sliding on their hind feet in the loose gravel they made jumps and recovered to slide some more. At last, on the flats, they rushed toward the smoking gates. Through the first veil of burning wood, they came into the acrid cloud of black powder smoke. With what they knew about the layout from interrogating Watrous about the place, Slocum pointed up the clogged street of upset carts, dead animals and bodies. It was tough to rein around all the obstacles, but the main part of the fort was in the back, according to their information.

Slocum banished his pistol in case. The red kerchief tied like garters on their arms was supposed to make them a part of the invaders. But the fierce house-to-house fighting on either side made him wonder about the effectiveness of their uniform.

Several soldiers were shooting at the last building from behind an overturned wagon. Slocum stepped down from his horse and tied his with the Chief's to a *carreta*.

"Think he is standing them off?" Chief asked as they hurried to join the soldiers.

"His men maybe, but I'd bet a twenty-dollar gold peso, he's not here."

"Where could he go?"

"Like smoke," Slocum said and the Apache nodded. He knew all about that.

The non-com in charge of the attackers was giving orders where to shoot. When one of the bandits returned fire they all shot at that window.

"You're too late," Slocum said. "Shoot at each window. Then they won't get a chance to shoot and you can get some men in closer."

The man smiled and nodded, calling out names of men to go ahead when they began the barrage. He directed them to points they needed to be.

"When they get there, hold their fire until you say so and they can cover for the next wave to move up."

"Ah, *si*, senor" the sergeant said, pleased. "Fire at all the windows. Now!"

In less than fifteen minutes the resistance melted and Slocum crossed the threshold of El Maldito's headquarters. The remaining outlaws, hands in the air, coughing, some bloody, but hands raised, came out.

Slocum stopped a man who looked like he might have been in charge. "Keys to the jail."

"We have no jail."

Slocum jammed his Colt in the man's guts. "Your life ain't worth two centavos. Tell me where the keys are or you die now!"

"All right. All right."

With a candle lamp in one hand and his six-gun in the other, he shoved the man ahead of him going down the stairs into a dungeon cut out of stone. Water dripped nosily in places.

Slocum held up the light at the first iron bars. Eyes in the darkness flickered in the light. Bearded skeletons of men dressed in soiled rags struggled to their feet.

"Mother of God, you came to save us," one cried.

"Yes. Juan! Benito!" he called out. The stench of human waste and death fouled the stuffy air.

"Senor Slocum, back here," Juan called out as Chief unlocked the cell doors and spoke to the incarcerated men.

"Is Benito here?" Slocum asked. No one answered. Soldiers were beginning to help evacuate the ones that couldn't walk.

"Oh, senor," Juan cried. The tears ran down his face. "I thought I was going to die down here."

"You hear of man calling himself Benito?"

A man with a long beard being helped by a soldier stopped him. "I think they tortured him to death. Is your name Slocum?"

"Yes, how long ago?"

"A few days ago. He said tell Slocum I told them nothing."

"I won the bet," Slocum said hours later as he and Chief walked back to their horses with Juan.

"Yes, he wasn't there all right. But we know you wounded him," Chief said, from the information extracted from the bandits.

"It only makes the rattler more deadly."

"But he has lost his army, much of his riches and his fort," Juan said.

"But he'll regroup and fight again."

"The pack train was gone, too," Chief said.

"I'd bet they're off making another whiskey run to the border."

"So the ones you wanted the most—the packers and El Maldito—are together?" Juan asked.

Slocum nodded slowly. "They could be." He glanced over and shared a nod with the Apache.

"They'll be in your country, Chief," Slocum said, stepping in the saddle and offering Juan a hand up.

"I knew they would be going there. But I wondered about my vision."

"Where?" Slocum asked, checking the horse who resented a second rider and shuffled around under him. "Get your heels out of his flank."

"I am. I am," Juan said, clinging to his shoulders.

At last, the pony settled some and they rode out of the ransacked fort. Soldiers came to doorways and waved bottles at them, shouting, "Viva Mexico!" Under their arms were the camp followers of the bandits—to the victor always go the spoils. The night after a bandit dicked them, a horny *federale* would try to wear out the same hole.

At Leona's, she rushed out to hug her hired man, asking a thousand nonstop questions. At last she whipped the shawl tight around herself and looked up at Slocum.

"Neither the army—nor you—got him?"

"No, he wasn't there when we blew in his front door."

"What now?"

"We'll have to look elsewhere."

She nodded like she understood. "Come and eat. Maria has much food prepared."

Chief nodded at Slocum over the matter and he agreed. El Maldito had waited this long; he could wait longer.

"A telegram came for you," she said sashaying over to the stand in the door. She handed the yellow paper to him.

SLOCUM—NAMES I HAVE—REYAS—ANTONIO—
MONTOYA—MOB HUNG THEM OTHERS THE NEXT DAY—
HOLDEN.

Slocum nodded to the chief when he completed reading it. "We have three names for the smugglers in on the killing."

"Who are they?"

"Reyas, Antonio and Montoya. A lynch mob hung the ones I sent back the next day. You know any of them?"

The chief shook his head.

"We'll find them."

"Be good thing." He fell in behind Slocum as they headed for the dining table.

"Did you find the man that was missing, too?" she asked as she showed them where to sit.

"No, Maldito had killed him, they thought." Slocum began to fill his plate from the vast spread on the table.

"What did the colonel say?" she asked.

"He was pleased to have the bandit chief out of power. I guess he liked my military strategy, too. We blew in the front door and took the place with a minimum loss of lives."

"He is a good man."

"For a *federale* officer, not bad."

"You think that this bandit has gone to join the others?"

"He may have gone to find the smugglers. We took out his camp in the Madres and he knows that by now. So Chief and I think he's gone north."

"Wasn't he wounded?"

"They said he was, but I suspect he's only scratched."

"I wish you could stay longer." She turned her brown eyes at him in a begging fashion.

"Maybe next time."

"Oh, well, you always say that. Chief, come see me anytime." The Apache nodded, busy eating like a famished wolf.

Slocum and Chief left her house at sundown, both men weary, but anxious to get on the track again. They could ride till midnight or later and then catch a few hours of shut-eye. So they could catch up with the killers and get this over with, was what Slocum planned.

17

At dawn, the two rode into the mission at San Augustine. The bells were chiming for those to come to mass. Families hurried on foot in the coolness to accept the body and blood of Jesus Christ. Women with their heads wrapped in scarves did not look up at the two men's passage. Clinging to precious crosses and beads, they looked determined to take part in the ritual.

"Good morning, my sons," the padre said, standing in front of the brown adobe plaster church.

"Good morning, Padre. We are looking for some packers with big mules. Have they passed this way?"

"You know these men?" the priest asked with an edge of suspicion in his voice.

"Well enough," Slocum said. "Montoya, Reyas and—" He turned in the saddle and asked Chief, "That other one's name is Antonio?"

The Apache nodded. "That was his name."

Satisfied, the priest said, "They came by yesterday going to the border."

"Good, we can catch them by tonight."

"I am certain you can. They will camp at the Pipe Springs tonight."

Slocum checked with his man who dismissed any concern about the place or location with a pursed-lip look.

"*Gracias*, Padre." He reined his horse aside and touched his hat to the priest.

"*Vaya con Dios*," the man of God said and showed them the silver cross as a send-off blessing.

When they were near the outskirts of the mission's vineyards and irrigated orchards, Slocum turned in the saddle. "You know this place, Pipe Springs?"

"Bad place for Apaches. Once they poisoned many of my people there and took their hair."

"Scalpers, huh?"

"Yes, but the Apache God Ussen got even."

"How's that?" Slocum asked riding stirrup to stirrup with him.

"Caused big ground to shake and their springs dried up."

"Earthquake," Slocum said and nodded that he knew about them. Many places on the border had felt them. Springs between the Huachuca Mountains and Tombstone that never went dry, shut completely off. Whole villages along the border were left in shambles by the fierce seismic activity that rumbled and roared off and on for two years in northern Mexico and southern Arizona.

"Is there water there now?"

"Some."

"Good," Slocum said, looking across the heat waves that blurred the desert. "We'll need some."

In late afternoon, Chief pointed to the hills to the east. "There is Pipe Springs at the foot of them."

The desert escarpment stood a few hundred feet high and the eroded red sandstone looked like pipes through Slocum's brass telescope. But he could see little else. If they were there, he had no intention of riding in and getting shot up.

"Let's rest in one of these dry washes and check it out come dark."

Chief agreed and they rode up a deep one with high straight banks and some lacy shade from a few tough mesquites.

Their blankets rolled out and horses hobbled, they lounged till past sundown. Then they rolled the blankets up, tied them on behind their cantles and rode in to see what they could find out. Slocum let the Apache lead the way to the settlement, since he knew the area.

Al last, they hitched their horses and on foot, drew closer to the outline of hovels. Chief signaled for him to stay there, then drew a knife from a scabbard on his belt. With the stealth of a cat, he soon pounced on an unsuspecting victim.

"Mother of God!

"Hush or die," Chief ordered and held the knife to the man's throat as he pinned him belly-down on the ground.

"Don't kill me. Don't kill me," the man hissed.

Slocum moved closer, his six-gun in his fist. He searched the night, but heard only some voices talking farther away in the village.

"Where are the packers?' Chief asked his prisoner.

"Over there."

"How many?"

Slocum listened close.

"I don't know—"

Chief jerked him by the collar and laid the knife's edge to his neck.

"Four, five."

"Are Reyas, Antonio and Montoya there?"

"*Si.*"

"El Maldito?"

"Who?"

"Their boss."

"Reyas is the boss."

"Is there a black-bearded big man with them?" Slocum asked, looking around for any sign of movement or possible threat out in the silver starlight.

"No."

In the dim light, he and the Apache shared a disgusted scowl. Slocum nodded and holstered his gun. The leader had done something else, besides what Slocum had figured he would do. That meant he went back to the Madres to heal—damn!

"We'd better round up this bunch and take them to Bisbee."

"What about him?" Chief put away his knife, but still pinned him to the ground with his knee in the middle of his back.

"I swear—"

"Shut up. Tie and gag him." Slocum slid off his kerchief and knelt to tie it like a bit through the man's mouth. Chief produced some rawhide string. Soon the man's hands and feet were tied with his knees bent so he couldn't get up.

"You make a sound and you're dead," Chief said in his ear.

The response was a muffled, "Mmmm . . ."

They moved out into the darkness. Slocum went to the right and Chief to the left. Moving with care around some dark, still jacals, Slocum closed in on the campfire. A guitar picker was strumming a song and hands clapped to the music. Some yells of encouragement came from the sides. Rounding a corner, Slocum caught sight of their heads and quickly drew back from the firelight. He expected what he saw: a girl dancing in the fire-light with a tambourine that she used to keep time.

Grateful for the distraction, he peered around the edge until he could count five men busy clapping their hands in time with the dancing. She was showing off to them, wagging her hips, tossing her wild hair and shaking her breasts to the music.

"Hands high or die!" Slocum shouted, stepping out with his gun in his hand.

Wide eyes turned to look at him in shock. One of the packers broke and dove for his rifle, but he never made it. A moccasin-clad foot stomped his forearm to the ground and he looked up bug-eyed at Chief's new Colt in his face.

The dancer melted and the one strumming the guitar threw up his hands, too, though Slocum doubted that he was one of the packers.

"Who's Reyas?"

"Me," the shorter one of them said. A burly built man of forty, his eyes showed his hatred and anger over being jumped in camp.

"Antonio?"

A big mustached one nodded and stood up. His diamond eyes cut through the swirling smoke and his anger burned the night.

Slocum nodded. After Chief purged him of weapons, Slocum moved him with a wave of his gun barrel to stand with Reyas. "Now who's Montoya?"

"I am Montoya." A short man rose and stepped forward.

"You shoot my Apaches in the back of the head?"

"No, no, senor."

"Who did?" Slocum looked over at the other packers for their reaction.

"Not us," Reyas said in his tough way.

"You three were the only ones who could have done it."

Reyas shrugged off his words. "Someone else must have. Not us."

"No, a *bruja* told me you shot them in the back of the head in a dry wash."

A scowl of disbelief swept over Reyas's dark face painted red by the firelight. "How would she know that?"

A rifle shot cut the night. The girl screamed and Slocum hit the dirt. The outlaws scattered like quail into the inky darkness. Where was the shooter? Slocum heard the chief's six-gun bark and a man scream. Two more rifle rounds plowed into a nearby jacal and each sent up a cloud of dust from the impact that boiled in the fire's red blaze.

"He's too far out," Slocum said to his own man off to his left after seeing the last orange muzzle blasts by the sniper. Loud maniacal laughter filled the night. To Slocum's disgust, the packers were getting away. He could hear the milling of hooves and mules snorting. The madman with the rifle, laughing at them out in the night was El Maldito; they'd struck them too soon.

"I got one of them," Chief said, bellying down beside him.

Slocum nodded. "I'm more concerned they're getting our horses."

"Be a long damn walk home."

"A long one. Let's see who you shot. Keep down, he's still out there." Staying out of the fire's light, they slipped across to the body. Slocum turned him over. "It's Antonio."

"I was hoping it was Reyas," Chief said, squatted a few yards away, balancing a rifle over his knees.

"He's one of the tough ones. We still have him, Cortez and Maldito and two from the pack train left."

Chief bobbed his head in agreement. "I'll go see about the horses."

Slocum searched around in the night, satisfied the outlaws had fled. "I'll go, too. Wait." He searched the man's pockets, finding a small amount of money and removed his gun and holster. They might need all of it before they were through.

18

The desert picked no favorites. Bleached bones of men and animals littered the ground beside the wagon tracks filing north through the stunted greasewood toward some saw-edged mountains in the distance. But the line of them faded in and out of view in the dizzy heat waves that radiated off the bright tan ground. Animal and even human skeletons picked clean by sharp beaks and teeth. Then the ferocious red ants polished off the rest until even hair did not remain to identify them. No quarters here for the unprepared, the cowardly and the stupid.

The burro Slocum rode proved spirited enough to trot without much persuasion. The Chief's gray one needed more quirting to keep up in spurts. Either way they were on the mule tracks and Slocum counted that for something. The old saddles they found were not much good but they beat riding bareback. From their tracks the packer train appeared to headed for the States. Maldito must be wanting to make a big robbery to replenish his losses. The only place he could get a big take was Tombstone or the mines at Bisbee, which were closer. If Slocum judged wrong, he would miss him, but if they took a shortcut to Bisbee they might beat him to the mining town.

"Can we cut across and beat them on these donkeys to Bisbee?"

"Why would they go there?" Chief frowned.

"Get more money to replace his losses. Either rob banks or the mines."

"You think he's gone crazy?"

"I think he's been crazy. No normal man laughs like that."

"Bad sign, huh?"

"Bad sign."

Chief pointed to the north. "I know a small rancher who has an Apache wife. He may let us have horses."

"Now you're talking my language." Slocum let his burro trot off in the direction the Apache pointed.

In late afternoon they rode up into a small canyon and found an empty ramada and some pens.

"No one home," Slocum said disgusted, squeezing the saddle horn hard in his grip.

With a Spencer rifle at his waist, a hatless man stepped out of the mesquite. "Why do you come here?"

"We need some horses," Chief said, jumping down and shaking his head. "Pedro, this is *mi amigo*, Slocum."

"Why did you come here?" The man still looked uncertain at them.

"You know me I am Black Wolf. You are married to my granddaughter."

"Yes, but why did you come here?"

"Bandits stole our horses. We could only catch some burros or walk."

Pedro still acted mad over their intrusion. "And now they will follow your tracks up here."

"They don't know where we are. We're following them."

"I have a wife and two small children, we must live like coyotes up here. They will look for us. They steal my cattle that get out of the hills and I am a poor man."

Chief held up two brown fingers. "We need two horses."

"You have a hundred dollars to buy them?"

"I have about twenty dollars and you can get the rest from the mine man Duke Holden at Bisbee. I'll make you a note for the rest."

Pedro shook his head. "He would only laugh at me. What else do you have?"

Chief shook his head. "I have a pure silver cross that my grandson wore."

"I need money, not jewelry."

"It is pure silver." Chief handed it to him.

"How did an Indian boy get such a valuable thing?"

"Raiding I guess."

Pedro looked over the cross then he hefted it in his hand. "Heavy enough to be made of lead."

"No, it is silver."

"To give two good horses for twenty dollars—"

"Wait." Slocum threw a leg over the horn and jumped down. "I have a six-gun and holster in my saddlebags."

Pedro's eyes lighted up.

Thirty minutes later, they were mounted on snorty horses. Chief rode a gray and Slocum a long-headed bay. The bay tried to buck, but Slocum kept his head up with the bridle he'd made using an old cavalry bit that the woman brought him and some braided sisal string for his head stall since they had no leather. Makeshift and make-do, they rode in a long trot for the border in higher style than they rode in on.

"When will we get to Bisbee?"

"Maybe tomorrow." Chief shrugged and booted his lazy horse to keep up.

"No, we need to get word to warn them. Maldito might try something as soon as he gets up here."

"These horses don't have wings."

"You're right. We need to trade these for some real horses."

"Where can we steal them?"

"I'm not sure beg, borrow or steal, but we need some better ones."

"I know of no more ranches till we get to the Mule Shoes."

"Sam Davis," Slocum said. "He'll let us have some fresh ones."

"But he is up there."

"Make these boom-tails lope," Slocum said. "I want to be at Sam's by dark."

Chief looked at him, then went to booting his gray harder.

19

Sam Davis's place was nestled on Rye Creek, an intermittent stream with spring-fed potholes. High up in the live oak and juniper, his windmill stood against the starry sky and creaked away on the night wind. A couple of big Airedales came barking and growling at their approach.

Slocum stopped short of the big tank that mirrored the night. A steady stream of water gurgled out of the pipe into the tank. "Sam Davis! Slocum out here. Call off the dogs!"

Someone began to whistle and the stiff-legged dogs sniffing around their horses bounded off to their master.

"What in the hell are you doing up here this time of night?"

"Wish I had more time, but some outlaws we've been chasing are heading for the border."

"Border? You just came across it." The big man had his arms crossed holding a rifle.

"They're coming out of Mexico and going to rob something up here."

"Well, get down and tell me all about it."

"I would, but Chief and I need two good horses to ride. These crow baits aren't much to make time on."

"Hell, come on. I've got some good horses."

"That's Black Wolf," Slocum said over his shoulder as they headed for the pens.

"Evening," Sam said to him and set the rifle down against

127

the rails. He took a lariat off the post and the corral gate creaked open so he could slip inside. The swish of the rope cut the night air and a horse was stopped in his tracks. Sam handed the rope to Slocum for him to lead the captured one out of the pen.

"The mine will pay you for them," Slocum said as Sam took down another lariat and went after one more.

"Good, I could always use some cash," Sam said, laughing as he spoke to the second catch out of the herd. "You're lucky I had them up. I was going to turn this bunch out in the morning."

"Appreciate it," Slocum said, transferring the old saddle to his new horse.

"Who are these bandits?"

"Maldito is the leader."

"Tough hombre. How did you and grandfather get together?" Sam motioned to the old man.

"Maldito's gang killed two Apaches that were scouting for me," Slocum said, filling in some details as he completed girthing the stout horse.

Pushing open the gate, Sam gave the lead to Chief and nodded. "Here."

"Beats stealing them," the old man said with a grin in the starlight.

"Getting paid for them does, too." Sam chuckled. "You ever steal any of my horses?"

Chief shook his head and grunted, heaving the Mexican saddle on the pony. "A boy once stole a big blue roan from you. He bucked off everyone and they finally gave up riding him."

"He came home, too, after that," Sam said. "And six weeks later a bunch with Geronimo stole him."

"He ever come back that time?" Chief asked drawing up his girth.

"No."

Chief nodded as if he knew the outcome. "I think they tried to eat him when they couldn't ride him."

"Was he tough?"

"Too tough to eat, too." Both men laughed.

Slocum swung a leg over the back of the bay horse and checked him. "Here. Duke Holden at the mine will pay you."

The rancher accepted the note. "Be careful. I'd hate to lose a customer. Next time stay a while and visit."

"Promise," Slocum said and the two headed out in the night under the spray of stars.

The golden sun's rays came over their shoulders as they rode up the canyon into Bisbee. Donkeys brayed under their various loads: firewood sticks, water, milk, produce. Small fires on the edge of the street heated the vendors' stoves.

Moving through the congestion on horseback, Slocum and Chief headed uphill for the courthouse. Maybe they were still in time to stave off any attempt at robbery. Slocum stopped at the base of the courthouse stairs, dismounted and handed the reins to Chief.

"I'm going to see if Marshal Madden is here."

Chief agreed with a nod, twisting around in the saddle to appraise the deep shadows of the canyon and the tall buildings around him.

On the top landing Slocum went through the frosted glass door and started down the hallway. He located Madden, who was busy filling out a report under a lamp in his office.

"Huh, you back?" The man jerked up and frowned.

"I hope in time."

"For what?" Straight pen in his hand, Madden stretched and yawned.

"Maldito and his bunch are on their way to rob the banks."

"Huh?"

"I figure they're already here."

Madden's eyes narrowed in disbelief. "Here in Bisbee?"

"Here or in Tombstone, but I figure they'll try here first."

"Damn—" Madden jumped up and slapped on his brown hat. "We better roust up some help." In the hall, he shouted and a face appeared down the way. "We got trouble, ring the bell."

"Fire?"

"No worse, bank robbers."

"I'll ring it right away. Reckon they can hear it at the mine?"

"Send someone over to tell Duke Holden what's up." Madden turned back to look at Slocum. "Which bank will they try?"

"Which one is closest to getting out the back way?"

"The Grand Bank is two blocks west of here."

"I'm headed for that one," Slocum said. "Send others to the second bank."

"I'll be right along. You got a shotgun?"

Slocum shook his head. "I'll need two."

"Got them," Madden indicated the office down the hallway. Both men rushed into the sheriff's office. A red-faced deputy rose and frowned at the bell ringing going on overhead.

"Break out some Greeners," Madden said. "We've got bank robbers."

"Oh, hell—" The man went to fumbling for his keys to undo the padlock. Madden was behind the counter and put two boxes of shells on the top.

After Slocum tucked the boxes in his vest, the deputy handed him two of the scatterguns. Then he gave him a hard nod. "Good luck."

"I'll be coming—" Madden said behind him as he hurried out the office door. At the outside door and on the landing, Slocum tried to see but the twists of the street cut off his view. He clambered down the steep steps. At the bottom, he tossed one of the shotguns to Chief and exchanged the reins for a box of shells.

In the saddle, Slocum broke open the double barrel and inserted two brass casings in the chambers. Then he stuffed his vest pockets with ammo. That done he nodded to Chief and they sent their horses clattering up the stone street.

The Grand Bank sign came into view. Half a block away their way was blocked by a pack train of donkeys. Slocum roared for them to clear the way, but in the confusion the animals began to mill, congesting the entire street. Over his shoulder the pealing bell in the top of the courthouse was ringing loud, adding to the confusion of braying jackasses and the rest.

Then the notion struck Slocum. This burro train was a planned way to keep him away from the bank.

"Get down!" he shouted at the old man.

Seconds later, the sharp report and gun smoke from the bank's front door split the air. On his feet, Slocum dodged a bucking donkey gone wild. He wished for a rifle. The range was too great for the buckshot, but he'd lost his long gun when Maldito stole their horses. Might be his own gun being used up there at the bank to shoot at him for all he knew. He pressed his shoulder to the brick front of the building and tried to see the shooter.

One by one, the donkeys were fleeing downhill and the street was clearing. Still the rifleman in the bank's doorway controlled things in the street. No doubt giving the rest of the bandits time to clean out the vault, which ground on Slocum's thoughts as the bell ringing continued. Damn everyone must have heard it by then.

Another bullet ricocheted off the brick facing above his head. Slocum ducked and drew back.

"There's an alleyway behind these buildings," he said over his shoulder to Chief.

"How we get there?"

"Break in that store right here. We'll go out the back."

Chief nodded and used the shotgun's butt plate to shatter the glass. Slocum reached inside and undid the latch. They hurried through the dark room that smelled of yard goods and leather shoes. He used his boot on the back door and shattered the latch. In seconds the two were in the narrow alley scattering half-wild cats as they ran up the confines between the bluff and the back of the businesses.

Ahead Slocum could hear the drum of retreating hooves on the solid rock base. *Too late* crossed his mind. He ran harder and burst on the scene as two men ran out of the rear of the bank slinging lead at them.

He paused, put the double barrel to his shoulder to aim the shotgun. The rapid fire of both barrels was punctuated by two more. Loose horses exploded and both men went down.

Wary more might rush out, Slocum broke the smoking shotgun apart, jerked out the empties and reloaded. With a click of the action closing, he looked out over the rubbish-piled space ready for another sign of resistance.

He reached the two wounded men lying on the ground and dared to peek in the bank. Blood all over made the floor look like a slaughter plant. A man wearing a green visor half sat up with his back to the counter. Life gone from his dull eyes, he stared into eternity at his low cut shoes. Slocum stepped over his feet and looked ahead. A balding man with gunshots dotting his back lay facedown on the trail to the open bank vault, his white shirt now scarlet from his fatal wounds.

A pair of lace-up shoes stuck out from the edge of the nearby desk and a heavy wool skirt was hiked high enough to show a woman's dark stockings. Her long brown hair had come loose from her bun, veiling her death-pale face; she looked to be in her thirties. A black hole in her forehead marked the fatal wound.

"Oh, dear Jesus—" Madden said, coming in the front door.

Slocum put the shotgun down on the desk and shook his head. "It doesn't get any better. Sorry, I tried to get back here in time."

"Oh, they might have robbed both banks if you hadn't warned us."

Slocum nodded. "They intended to, I am certain."

"They've run back to Mexico."

Slocum agreed.

"Damn, oh, damn," Holden said, coming in the doorway.

"He tried to get here and warn us," Madden said, indicating Slocum.

"Thirty minutes too late," Slocum said.

"I'll have to go after them," Holden said.

"They'll be in Mexico," Madden said.

"Mexico be damned. I either get them or I lose my job."

"We'd better get what information we can out of those two in the alley that the Chief and I shot," Slocum said.

"You do that. I'm forming a posse. I need to get after them."

"I'm not saying you're right or wrong, but the dust of a posse will only drive them farther away and make them harder to catch," Slocum said.

"You said that the last time," Holden said, sharply enough to emphasize his point.

"I lost some good men trailing them. And I sent a couple to hell. You go to Mexico and find out how tough they are to run down."

"What do I owe you for the ones you ran down?"

"Make it easy on yourself."

Holden piled some gold double pesos on the counter. "Two hundred enough?"

Slocum nodded. "Pay Sam Davis for the two horses and we're even."

"I'll pay him."

"Good," Slocum said and turned to Holden. "There's the shotgun on the desk. Chief bring that one over here."

The Apache set it down and emptied his pockets.

"I guess our part is over," Slocum said to him.

His sun-wrinkled face bobbed up and down under that strange straw sombrero. "Goddamn good deal. My ass is sore from riding horses."

"Damn, I wish Holden hadn't done that," Madden said. "You got that first bunch. Guess he's scared of losing his job. But no one could predict . . . damn you came on the run."

"Let's go see what those out back have to say—"

Chief shook his head. "Both dead."

"Well," Slocum said in disgust. "That's over. I'm going to find a place to sleep. We ain't had much of that lately."

Chief nodded in agreement as the open front door filled with the curious.

"Get back! Get back!" Madden demanded, waving them out of the way to allow him and Chief to slip by them. "This is the business of the law. Get out of the way. Anyone seen the coroner?"

Slocum and the Apache found their horses and led them to the livery. "I'm going to find a bed," he said to the Apache.

"Good. I be here with horses when you ready."

"Ready?" Slocum blinked at him. "I'll pay you part of this money now."

Chief shoved his hand back. "Posse never get them." His head bobbed and he grinned. "You and me, we get them."

Pained, Slocum looked at the brown face and the dark eyes slanted at the corners. Hellfire, the old man was serious. Slocum could see he wasn't getting off this easy yet. Not till Joe and Black Wolf's killers were dead.

"Daylight," Slocum said, then looked up for the sun time. But he couldn't see it for the two story buildings over them.

"I be ready."

"I guess we can find a packhorse and some supplies in the morning."

Chief held out his palm.

Slocum put five of the gold cartwheels in his hand.

"Be ready."

"Thanks," Slocum said, reset the six-gun on his hip and headed up the street. He drew a breath before he climbed the stairs and knocked.

"I am sorry, senor," the Mexican maid said, holding the door half shut. "We are closed."

"Lucille's expecting me," Slocum said, moving the door open wider.

"But the senora said—"

"She'll know who I am. Thanks."

"What is your name, senor?" she asked.

"Slocum," he said, stepping in and heading through the parlor for the hallway. Light-headed with lead-filled eyelids, he knocked and then turned the knob. Lucille looked up to sling her hair back from her face. Then a smile of recognition spread over her and she unflexed her bare legs and crossed the room to welcome him.

Who needed sleep anyway?

20

Face in his palms, Slocum scrubbed his whiskers and sat on the edge of the bed. The hangover from his long-awaited sleep had caught up with him. In the flickering candlelight of the room he looked around for her, and finally twisted to see her fetal form curled up in the bed asleep behind him.

Still not fully awake, he rose and went to the window. The street below was deserted and dark. Thoughts of the long ride south again felt impenetrable to him. This Maldito was more like a spirit than a person—they'd blasted his fortress and he'd escaped. Captured his men and he came to save them. Murdered people in the bank robbery like a madman. And what about Mary and his friend Richardo and this bandit they called Scar? Damn, the whole world was upside down.

Seated on the chair, he pulled on his boots and looked across the small room at the woman of the night—Lucille. Far better to stay in her arms than set out for this endless ride into the hot desert looking for killers made of smoke. But the old man under the strange-looking straw hat would be waiting for him. He bent over and kissed her on the smooth cheek.

Angel of love, sleep well—I will be back. Placing a golden double eagle on the bed beside her, he straightened and put on his gun belt. On his toes, he left her to her dreams and moved out of the quiet house for the livery.

He woke the hustler. "Is Chief here?"

"I guess—" The man sat up and yawned. "He was when I turned in."

"I'll find him. Go back to sleep."

"Hell, I'm up now."

Slocum found Chief saddling his horse when he walked back in the sour piss-smelling stables.

"You finally came," the old Apache said and chuckled like he knew when Slocum would be ready to ride out.

"Got a packhorse?"

"All of it is over there." Chief pointed and led his horse out of the the stall.

"Good."

"They won't be far below the border."

After brushing the bay's back clean, Slocum slapped on the worn pad and the dried-up saddle he had found in Mexico inside an empty jacal. "I suppose you saw him in a vision?"

Chief nodded. "Not far."

The hustler, looked skeptically at Chief in the flickering light of the lantern. "You see lots of things in visions?"

Chief stopped smoothing the pad on the pack mule's back. "Sometimes."

"How do they come to you?"

Chief shook his head as if he had no answer. "Ussen tells me what he wants me to know."

"Damn, I wish someone would tell me something like that."

"Maybe tell you when you will die?"

"Oh, hell, no, I don't want to know that." The man's shoulders shook underneath his shirt at the notion.

"Then you'd better not wish for such things."

"Lordy, I won't ever ask for it again. You imagine that— knowing the day death was coming after you."

Slocum nodded with grim set to his mouth. "It comes a lot for me."

"Hell, you two done ruined my day or night, whatever it is. That makes me sick thinking about it now."

Slocum stepped up in the saddle. "It's only dreams."

"Yeah, but what if they work out like that?"

"You'd be dead, so what would it matter?" He winked at Chief, ducked his head for a low purlin and rode out in the street. Chief brought the mule on. The clop of hooves echoed up and down the narrow street until they were far up Tombstone Canyon and topped out in Mule Shoe Pass. Then, with a cool night wind in their faces, they dropped off the mountain and headed through the ghostly shapes of the junipers for the Santa Cruz bottoms.

Dawn found them across the border, following the tracks in the tan dust that pointed southward along the water course. Slocum heard the pop of a distant rifle.

"Holden may have them cornered."

Chief nodded.

"You bring the mule. I'll go ahead and see what's happening." He set the bay in a long lope and soon reached the ridge where he could look across the tall cactus-studded flats. The shooting was farther south and sporadic. He doubted they had the bandit leader. No doubt some of Maldito's men had been left to slow them, so the posse would grow tired and quit him. They were not dealing with a fool.

He reined up the bay when he could see the dots of smoke. The bandits held the high ground and would be hard to assault from the front. Viewing the battle, he wished for field glasses when Chief rode up and handed him an old pair.

Slocum nodded in approval. "You did well."

Sitting their horses, he scanned the area. If they could skirt west, come in behind them and cut off their chance to run off, they'd have them.

"Can we—"

Chief nodded even before he got the words out. "Go west, ride up the lowlands and circle back in."

"Lead the way."

They swept west and soon dropped into a great swale that ran southward. Slocum beat on the mule to make him keep up and they made good time on the alluvial fill. Higher up rocks would have hurt their progress, but this area was easy to cross in a high lope. They'd gone several miles, when Chief pointed to a clef in the ridgeline on their left.

Slocum nodded and they pulled their tired horses down to a jog. Hot and sweaty, the horses bobbed their heads and the mules snorted in the dust in complaint. Chief pushed his pony to the top of the rise and they could hear more shots.

Slocum nodded in approval. They were behind the fight.

In a short while, Chief halted, slipped from his horse and handed him the reins.

"I will get their horses. They are in the next dry wash. When I yap like a coyote, come over the ridge and then we can close in on them."

"Be careful," Slocum said, dismounting and pulling down the crotch of his pants.

Chief never answered, but left in a low run through the catclaw and cactus. Slocum squatted on his boot heels and waited. Shortly, he saw the chief's head appear and he came leading a familiar mount and rig with three others. It was the horse that Leona had given him and his saddle.

"You didn't yap," he said, busy inspecting his things including the silver-mounted Smith and Wesson pistol still in the saddlebags.

"No need to. There was no guard."

"Well, let's take them." Slocum checked the cinch and swung in his own saddle. It felt good after the curled up hull he'd ridden down there in. He tested the horn and laughed aloud. "Never figured I'd ever see it again."

"Hobble them in the next wash?" Chief asked.

"Good idea."

The horses hobbled, they set out in the direction of the occasional shots. Slocum carried the silver pistol in his waistband. He really would have liked a .44/40 or a .38/40 but there were none on the ponies.

"We get a rifle from one of them," Chief said as he moved out through the catclaw.

"Yes," Slocum agreed. A rifle would be a good thing in this fight.

They stopped and appraised the situation. From the shots, they located four of the shooters on the edge of the rise.

"Four?" Slocum whispered, holding up that many fingers.

Chief shook his head. And then he showed him five dark digits, including one that had been cut half off in some long ago accident or fight.

"Where's the last one?"

They searched and searched, then a rifle far to the right barked in rapid succession. He was purposefully off over there to thwart any chance when Holden's men tried to circle them.

"I'll get the guy on the left and we can get the rest of them one at a time."

Chief nodded.

Slocum set out easing his way forward until he got close enough to hear the man work the slide on his rifle. When he raised up to shoot, Slocum charged in and before he could reload, busted him over the head with his pistol. The bandit sprawled facedown and Slocum snatched his rifle.

It was a nearly new Winchester and there were still plenty of cartridges in his bandoliers. He stripped off the ammo belts, then took the sash from the man's waist and tied his hands behind his back. A strip off his shirt gagged him should he wake up, and his feet were tied with another piece of cloth.

Bandoliers over his shoulders, rifle in his hand, he felt like an ammo wagon headed uphill towards Chief, who was ready to take out the next one.

A couple of bullets whistled close by.

"They are getting to be better shots," Chief said.

"We'd better tell them who's up here."

"They can't get to their horses without running across the open ground," Chief pointed out.

Slocum agreed.

He used his hands to cup his mouth. "Holden! Holden! Hold your fire, we've got two of these bandits and can get the rest."

"Hold your fire. That you, Slocum?"

"It's me. We have three more left up here. I'm giving them thirty seconds to give up."

A sombrero appeared in the mesquite as the man rose up gun ready to shoot and his gun barked. The slug whizzed over their heads. But the round from Chief's rifle sent the bandit into a spin and then out of sight. Slocum kept his eye on the other locations, his rifle cocked and ready.

"Surrender or die!" Slocum shouted and the other two raised their hands and stood up.

"I will go see about the one I shot," Chief said and Slocum nodded.

"It's over. Holden, come on up and meet them."

He could hear the big man cussing as he rounded up his posse.

The men, an assortment of businessmen and miners, who

staggered up to the rise with Holden, all looked hollow-eyed and dust-floured. The entire operation had taken the heart out of them. Even as they rounded up the three bandits, it was obvious they were through.

"The sumbitch got away," Holden said as if hardly able to contain himself. "Oh, yeah, thanks. We'd have got them, but it would have taken hours."

"None of the original bunch from the store murder are here," Slocum pointed out. "Chief and I know them on sight. They might not even have been on this one, but we suspect they were."

"This damn Maldito—" Holden shook his head. "Who is he?"

"A powerful bandit with spiritlike qualities about him. I thought we had him when the *federales* stormed his fort. But he wasn't there."

"I know you've rode lots of horseflesh into the ground going after him, but he's got to be human." Squatting down on their heels, the two men talked apart from the others.

"Not in Mexico," Slocum said and took the cigar the big man offered.

"Aw, bullshit, there ain't no ghosts or spirits. Just superstitions and crap. I guarantee when we catch him, he'll have to shit just like the rest of us."

Slocum rolled the grit out of the corners of his mouth. "He's elusive as a shadow, but I agree he's human and has been lucky."

"So, what next?" Holden asked.

"If it was me, I'd send the posse home with the prisoners and go on. They won't stand much more and he's half a day or more ahead of you."

"What about you and the Injun?"

"Chief wants the three who killed his grandson and Maldito. Since you fired me I'm tracking along with him."

"Hell, you're both rehired."

Slocum stirred the dust with a twig. "I'll ask him."

"Why not, you may just as well be paid for it."

"Apaches are funny."

"Ask him. I'll send these boys home."

Slocum drew deep on the cigar, then he nodded as he exhaled. He pushed off his knees and went to find Chief. Better talk to his pard before he closed any deal.

Chief was sitting in the shade of a lacy mesquite, his back to the trunk, eating a fried pie. "Pretty good. Guy give me two. This is second one."

Slocum agreed and squatted down. "Holden will pay us to go along."

"What we'll do with all of them?" He indicated the posse men with the hand holding the half-eaten apple desert.

In a lowered voice, Slocum explained, "He's sending them home with the prisoners. Be the three of us, I guess."

Chief nodded he heard him and masticated on his treat.

"I figure we may as well get paid, huh?"

"Maybe speed up catching him, too."

"I'll tell him we'll go with him."

Chief nodded. "But where?"

"Damn good question. He has no base in Fronteras or in the Madres. A coyote on the run is harder to get than one with a den."

Chief nodded in agreement. "And he will be tougher."

No doubt in Slocum's mind about that—he'd be much harder to pin down.

21

They reached Ascension in two days. It was a small village in the foothills. Holden's horse needed a new shoe and they left their mounts and pack animals at the blacksmith's shop under a spreading cottonwood. At a small cafe, they sat outside under a brush arbor porch and the young girl waited on them.

"We have some fresh roasted *cabrito*," she announced.

The three nodded to each other in approval. "That, frijoles, flour tortillas and some *cerveza*," Holden ordered.

A smile spread over her small dark face. "I will bring it to you as soon as Maria has it ready and the *cerveza* is coming." She bowed and hurried back inside.

Small birds sang and the gentle breeze flowed across Slocum's face as he slouched in the wicker chair. He removed his hat to expose his head to the pleasurable air. Good at last to be in some place, away from the glaring desert for a brief respite.

"The blacksmith said the gang didn't stay long here." Holden went over the information they'd gathered.

"Sounded like they were trying to get somewhere quick on purpose to me," Slocum said, deep in thought about the many trails that led to this small community.

"What do you think, Chief?" Holden asked.

"He said he knew one man who rode with them—Antonio."

Slocum sat up when she brought the tall schooners of beer. "You thinking he lives around here?"

"Yes."

"How will we find him?" Holden asked.

Slocum clicked two gold double eagles in his fingers. "Money talks in these places."

"How do we post the reward?"

Slocum raised the glass of beer and nodded. "I'll go plant the idea after we eat."

"Then we'll stay the night here?" Holden asked over his beer, the foam on his mustache.

"Chief and I plan to."

Holden nodded in surrender.

The name of the man who Slocum found in the cantina was Obregon. He met Slocum and his partners in the alley and his dark eyes darted around like a cornered rat.

"—the woman he lives with. She had a jacal up this hill—" Out of breath, he held his hand to his chest and looked around in the starlight like a man under a death sentence. "He must never know—"

"He will never know."

"Oh, he would kill me so quick."

"He won't know," Slocum assured him in Spanish.

"Aye, I need the money so bad."

"We get him, you get paid," Slocum said, growing weary of the man's lamenting. Climbing the steep hill, he undid the tie-down on his Colt. Chief carried a rifle and Holden came behind as the rear guard in case of a trick. Something about the man made Slocum suspicious enough that he warned them they needed to be careful.

The jacal was dark. Slocum sent Chief around to the back. He and Holden squatted down to give the Apache time to get into place. Obregon paced in a small circle until his moves irritated Slocum to the breaking point.

"Sit down."

The man obeyed, but still fidgeted.

At last the *whit-whoo* of a quail call told Slocum his man was in place. He nodded to Holden and used a hand on Obregon's shoulder to get him to stay when they rose to go after the man. Slocum drew his Colt and they headed for the shack.

They stopped thirty feet from the building and spread out.

"Antonio, come out with your hands up," Slocum ordered in Spanish.

A woman's voice let out a small scream from inside the jacal.

"You are surrounded. Put your hands in the air and come out now!"

Slocum could hear someone scrambling around and a woman protesting. "Don't be loco."

He nodded at Holden that the man was going to fight. The cocked pistol in Slocum's grip, the seconds passed like long minutes. A cur dog yapped in the distance. Then there was the sound of boots running and shots behind the jacal.

"He's gone out the back way," Slocum said and pointed with his gun hand for Holden to take the far side.

When Slocum rounded the building, he saw the mine man, and down the hillside he could see the outline of the strange hat as Chief stood over someone on the ground.

A woman began to sob and cry out from the jacal. "You've killed my Antonio!"

When Slocum squatted down beside the prone outlaw, he struck a match, then he nodded. Unmistakably the dead one was the same face they saw in the firelight the night that Chief and he had captured the gang before Maldito rescued them.

Satisfied, Slocum holstered his six-gun and then held out his hand for the money to pay his man. He nodded to Chief he was ready to leave and started up the hill. A woman wrapped in a blanket avoided them and then rushed to her dead lover. When Slocum found Obregon, he held out his hand and Slocum paid him the two double eagles.

The man tried to peer in the dark. "Is he really dead?"

"Yes," Slocum said and headed back to the village.

Half stumbling as he looked over his shoulder, Obregon tried to stay close to them. The man no doubt was scared of some revenge that would be taken out on him.

"Any more bandits around here?" Holden asked him.

"No, ah, no—" the man mumbled. "He was the only one, but his gang will come looking for me."

"We won't tell them," Slocum said, anxious to get rid of the informer.

"What if they come back?"

"Let me know and I'll pay you more."

"No, I mean to kill me."

"That's what I mean. You tell me and I'll handle them."

"Oh!" the man moaned and hugged himself as if freezing. "They will come back and I will die."

Back at the livery where they had pallets laid in the hay, Holden laughed aloud. "Damn, I'm glad to be rid of that cry-baby, Obregon."

"Me, too," Slocum said, ready to pull on his covers. It would be cool by morning.

"Where's the Chief?" Holden asked.

"Off talking to his God." Slocum turned over and went to sleep.

Before sunup, they saddled and packed the mule and a big horse from Holden's string. Working in the predawn chill, Slocum used a thick blanket for a shawl to cut the cold. Their animals ready, they went to the cafe where the owner, a short, fat woman, had promised the night before to have breakfast ready for them.

She hurried out with steaming coffee mugs when they arrived and hitched their horses at the rack. The mule's raspy braying threatened to wake the entire village.

"So early," she scolded them, hustling around to deliver plates heaped high with scrambled eggs, chilies, beans and pork. Then she passed around another plate loaded with hot, fresh-made, flour tortillas.

The young girl kept their mugs full of steaming coffee and the three feasted.

"Lupe," Holden called out to her, "we would soon be too fat to ride if we lived here."

"Ah, you are good men," she said, drying her hands on her apron and rushing out to join them.

"Good men must ride on," Holden said and paid her.

"Gracias," she said and bowed to them. "Come and eat again with me some time."

They agreed and went to their mounts stretching and rubbing their full bellies. When they reached a dip in the hills and Slocum looked back at the cottonwoods and wondered if they would ever get any of the other killers. Maybe Chief had had another vision. With regret, he turned to face the hills ahead. He always hated to leave those little pockets of tranquility where life never moved faster than a burro's pace. But they, too, held their own brand of rattlesnakes like Antonio. At least he wouldn't kill again.

Two days later, they rode into Arroyo. Signs indicated they were close to the bandits. The horse apples proved fresher.

"What do you know of this place?" Holden asked as they rode three abreast.

"Just another place," Slocum said. "They once had a pretty girl that danced in that cantina up there."

"Let's go find her." A smile spread across Holden's face.

Slocum checked around. He had no intention of walking in on the bandits. No group of horses was at any hitch rack, nor had he spotted any in the alleys they passed. No sign the bandits were there, but he felt dissatisfied. They could be behind any corner, out of sight. A sharp edge rode in his mind as he dismounted and they headed for the batwing doors.

Inside the shadowy interior, he felt relieved—no gang members. Holden selected a table that would allow them to have their backs to the wall and they took chairs as the bartender came over to get their orders.

"What was her name, that girl who danced here?" Holden asked Slocum, who was leaning back in the chair, tapping his fingertips together.

"Donna."

"Ah, amigo, where is Donna?" Holden asked the short man in the white apron.

"Ah, you know her?"

"Where is she?"

"I will send a boy to get her."

"Good, do that and then bring us a bottle of your best and three glasses. When did Maldito leave here?"

"No savvy, Maldito, senor."

Holden flipped a double eagle in the air and caught it on his wrist. "Head or tails?"

"Aw, senor, I could not gamble for so much money."

"Is it an eagle or the flag?"

The man shook his head and looked to the other two for help.

"All you have to say is when he left here and the coin is yours."

The Mexican looked around the empty cantina. "At sunup."

"Where did he go?"

"You said—"

"Where did he go?"

"He did not say but he rode east—Campo, I think."

Holden laughed and tossed him the coin. "Now bring the bottle."

"I send for the girl, too."

"Do that, too," Holden said and shook his head.

"I go look around," Chief said and stood up. "Plenty time to drink later."

"Watch your backside," Slocum said.

"We hear shots we'll come running," Holden said and took the bottle from the man. "They drink lots of this horse piss?"

"Who, senor?"

"Maldito's men."

"They are very bad hombres."

"That's why we want them."

Slouched, Slocum sipped his glass of mescal slow. He watched a man come in, go to the bar, drink a beer, consider them and leave half his beer on the counter.

When the man slipped out, Slocum swung his feet out of the other chair. "They ain't all gone. Had one in here size us up."

"How the hell do you know that?" Holden demanded.

"Ain't no poor Mexican alive unless he has the shits and had to go to the crapper going to leave half a glass of beer that he paid for on the bar."

A glint of sun was shining through the mug and the container was over half full with pale yellow beer. Holden sat upright and quickly agreed.

"What did he look like?"

"Some peon they paid to scout us."

"How many you figure are out there?"

"What does he leave behind? A half dozen?"

Holden looked very sober as he slapped the cork back in the bottle. "What should we do about it?"

"Wait here. Chief may locate them for us."

"Or they find him."

"That old Apache didn't get that gray hair by not being cautious."

"I wonder—" Both men looked up as woman came in the back door talking a hundred miles an hour to a man with a guitar.

Slocum didn't get all she had to say, but when she came in the light, he could see her black eye and the rage in the other. She blinked her good eye at them. It was the look—who are you?

Holden removed his hat and bowed his head to her. "Good day, my lady. They say you are the best dancer in Sonora."

She put her hands on her hips and if she recognized Slocum, it was only for a second that recognition swirled through her hard glare at him. "I was afraid you were more of the *bastardos* that were here yesterday."

"They didn't all leave," Holden said looking hard at her.

She turned to the guitar man seated on a stool. "Did you hear him?"

He nodded and acted more interested in his instrument than answering her.

"Are they still in this village?" she demanded.

He shrugged and plunked on the strings.

"The black eye was a gift from who?" Holden asked, leaning back.

From the corner of his eye, Slocum saw the bartender take off his apron, wad it up and move down the bar toward the front door.

"Hey! Don't leave partner, cause when you go for that door, I aim to drop you in your tracks," Slocum said, scrapping the chair around to better view the situation. He placed the Colt on the tabletop.

"Donna, darling," Slocum drawled. "You and that picker get behind the bar. No rush. Walk over there and when the shooting starts, get down low."

"They coming in that way?" Holden asked.

"I'd judge the back one, since the barkeep was headed for the front one."

"We did not bring them here," Donna announced.

Slocum nodded he understood her. "Just get down when the shooting starts."

She agreed with a look of apprehension.

"I'll barricade that back door some so they can't simply kick it open," Holden said. "You keep an eye on the front."

"Got you covered." Slocum crossed his dusty boot over the other one in the chair seat before him.

Holden took two chairs and went to the back door. He hooked the first one under the latch and put the bar in place that locked it at night. Satisfied he came back and poured himself a drink. He offered Slocum some for his glass and he nodded.

"Hey, barkeep, how many are out there?" Holden asked, taking a seat and holding up the glass to look through it.

"I don't know, senor."

"Better go to thinking about how many there are. Your life may depend on it."

"No savvy?"

"Say four men rush the cantina and they get us, the last man may get you."

"There were four this morning," he said real fast.

"What does the guitar picker say?" Holden asked her.

"Tell him!" she ordered.

"Ramon Cortez is with them."

"Who in the hell is he?" Holden asked, scowling at Slocum.

"Maldito's brother-in-law," Slocum said and used his tongue to trace his molars. Must be a string of goat meat left in them. "He's a killer."

"He make four or five?"

The bartender shrugged. "I don't know."

"Four," the guitar player said. "They rode back here a couple of hours ago."

"You thought they had sent for me?" she asked him.

"I thought so."

"Who gave you the black eye—" Sounds of men running and dogs barking outside in the street drew Holden's questioning to a close.

Slocum dropped to his knees and took aim at the batwing doors. First bandit through them was a dead one. He dried his palm on his pants and retook the position of being ready.

Holden tossed his head toward the back. Two men were talking fast and coming around the building.

"Charge!"

The door parted. A gun hand first. Slocum squinted his right eye, aimed and fired. The room boiled with acrid black powder smoke. The gunman crumbled to the floor on the porch. He never moved. Two shoulders hit the back door. It held. Holden leveled his Colt at the door. Pouring five rounds of ammo into the thin wood, he sent the would-be invaders to hell.

On his feet, Slocum rushed to the front doors. The bandit lying on the porch had never moved. Slocum turned an ear. He thought he heard someone fighting with a horse. Outside in the bright light he saw the rider on the horse headed east. For a second, he thought the horse might toss his rider, but he managed to straighten him out and ride away.

Chief came on the run with his rifle, but by then the rider was too far away.

"Any more?" Slocum asked.

The Apache shook his head. "I found their horses when the shooting started."

"Who's horse was that?"

"Mine," said an angry hatless vaquero, sticking his head out the window above. "My good *caballo.*"

"We'll give you his horse."

"*Gracias*, but first I have more business up here."

Slocum heard the woman giggle and he knew that the upstairs was a cathouse.

"Them two out back are in pretty bad shape. Want to see if you know them?" Holden asked from the cantina's front doors.

"We're coming," Slocum said.

"I have their horses," Chief said as they came inside. "I need a big drink."

"On the table, help yourself," Holden said and turned to Donna. "And now, my lady, you can dance."

Slocum did not recognize either man in the alley. Another encounter with Cortez, Maldito must be taking them serious after all his pursuit. At his back, Slocum could hear the guitar strings and the crash of the castanets. Donna would be dancing for them. Good. That might take his mind off the killers. He needed a little escape.

22

"Who gave you the black eye?" Holden asked her as she sat with them at the table.

"Maldito." She tossed the hair from her face and raised her chin.

"Nice guy," Holden said, stopping short of taking another sip of mescal.

"I would like to be there when you catch him," she said through her white teeth. "I would cut off his *pechos* and sack." Her long brown hand making a slashing wave like a sword.

"I'll have to remember that," Slocum said and toasted her. "Some say he is myth."

"He is no myth. He is a madman."

Slocum nodded at Holden. "Chief and I had an engagement with him and I suspected then he was crazy. But also smart like a fox. He sends others to do the dangerous things unless he's pinned down."

"Where was he going next?" Holden asked. "Did he ever say?"

She whirled and looked at the guitar man who sat across the room strumming his strings. "Where did he go?"

"Campo, I think."

"How far is that?"

"Twenty miles, maybe more," Slocum said. He glanced over at the Apache.

Chief nodded his head. "Maybe we could come in from the Madres and surprise them."

"You mean ride in from the other side?" Holden narrowed his eyes at the Apache. At the Chief's nod, he smiled and nodded his head. "Best damn idea we've had today. Let's drink to that." He raised his glass and toasted. "To Maldito's demise—and his castration as well."

"Yes!" Donna shouted and clinked her glass to the others.

A woman brought them food. A pile of mesquite-smoke-flavored meat, a pot of frijoles, chili sauce, flour tortillas and some red bananas. The guitar picker joined them.

A man came inside, he wore a top hat and a red sash at his waist. His Prince Albert coat was worn and dust-stained. He removed the hat and looked very official.

"Pardon my manners, gentlemen. I don't mean to disturb your meal."

Donna pointed a half eaten burrito in her hand at him. "He is the mayor domo. Hienie is his name."

"Mayor Hienie," Holden said. "What can we do for you?"

"I am the law in this village."

"Fine," Holden said. "What do you need?"

"Who will pay for the burial of these three men?"

Holden shot a gaze at Slocum, who shrugged.

"What are the charges?"

"To dig the graves costs two pesos apiece. Then we must pay the padre for saying mass over them."

"I see."

"Then I must file a report about their death."

"Total price comes to . . . ?"

"Twelve dollars."

"Well—" Holden said, squeezing his chin. "That's lots of money to pay."

"But it is expensive to do all that, too."

"I guess we'd better pay him," Slocum said and winked at Donna.

She smiled back.

"Here," Holden said and handed the man a double eagle. "Keep the change."

"Oh, *gracias*, *gracias*, you are most generous."

"You may go now, Mayor. We're having a wake to grieve the loss of them."

"Oh." The man straightened to his full height of five eight, replaced the top hat and marched out the front door to the accompaniment of the guitar.

Chief sat up straight and looked around like his neck was stiff and everyone laughed. "Him big turkey, huh?"

"He's the boss here," Holden said and slouched down in his chair.

"He's also the law as well," Slocum put in.

"He's the law?" Holden looked in doubt.

"No, but he can arrest you, fine you and put you behind bars."

"That's good to know." Holden reached across the table and went to refilling glasses. "Now, we next take Campo."

Slocum checked around to be sure the bartender could not hear and leaned toward Holden. "We need to send someone in there to see if they're set up for us."

"Good idea, but who?"

Donna leaned forward. "Let me go. They know all of you now."

"You might get more than a black eye next time," Slocum said.

"I will go in as an old woman."

Holden nodded. "That means riding most of the night."

"I don't care," she said.

"Slocum?"

"It would be dangerous." He sat back in the chair and considered the risk.

"I could get a different hat," Chief said.

"That might work."

"I get a new hat and watch her."

"I'd feel a damn sight safer about her." Slocum glanced over for the mine man's input.

"Settled," Holden said and put ten dollars on the table. "Here, go buy yourself a new hat."

"Better go before he changes his mind," Chief said, picking up the money. He ambled out of the saloon's front doors and Slocum sat back.

"We have their horses for you to ride. The guitar man going?"
She nodded.

"I'd like a few hour's shut-eye," Slocum said and stretched his arms over his head. "Before we ride out."

Holden shook his head. "I couldn't sleep, I'm too uptight. You go ahead."

"You can sleep at my casa," Donna said.

"How do I get there?" Slocum asked.

She rose and gave a head toss. "Follow me. When will we leave?"

"Sundown all right?" Holden asked.

"Fine, we'll be back here."

On her heels, Slocum followed her out the bullet-riddled back door. Then with her carrying her skirt, she lead the way between two adobe buildings and then across a narrow street. In the next close corridor, she stopped and looked back. Satisfied, she looked up at Slocum.

"It has been a while."

"I thought that, too, when I saw you." He took her in his arms and kissed her. Fire and passion fumed from her sweet mouth and wild tongue. Her firm breasts pressed into him as his hands grasped the rock-hard half moons of her butt.

"Oh—" she cried, breaking away from him. "We'd better hurry to my casa."

He looked back and saw nothing.

She searched both ways at the next street and quickly led him across. "Who is this man with the money?"

"Duke Holden. He works for the big copper mine at Bisbee. They want Maldito and his killers."

She unlocked her green door with a key. Inside, she quickly shut it behind them and relocked it. "We need no surprises. And who is the Apache?"

"Black Wolf, we call him Chief. Maldito murdered his grandson and another Apache named Joe."

She removed his vest as she stood in front of him in the shadowy light of the room. He undid his gun belt and put it on the table. Then he kissed her and his hand sought one of her hard, tube-shaped breasts. She raised the hem of her blouse and he switched to feeling the other one. Her fingers flew undoing the buttons on his shirt.

"You have been away so long—" Her voice was a smoky challenge. "I thought you might be dead."

He toed off his boots as she undid his pants and plunged her hands in to knead his privates. The britches fell on his feet and he stepped out of them. She let him to a pallet, pulling him down after her. Moving her supple body underneath him like a swimmer, she spread her legs apart and scooted down to meet his aching erection. With her long fingers, she guided the head of his dick into her.

"Oh, yes, dear God—" she said in a deep whisper.

He pumped the great shaft deeper and deeper into her slick cylinder. She let out a sharp cry and threw her legs in the air, bowed her back and pulled him down on top of her.

With him at the bottom of her well, she swung her head from side to side in wild abandonment. Her raspy, "Yes, yes," encouraged him to pound her harder and faster. Then she locked her heels behind his knees and arched her back at him. A sharp clit began to scribe on the surface of his swollen dick as he plunged in and out.

She began to moan in pleasure. Her face was lost under a film of wild loose hair. Then her frantic efforts to rub her stick on his became so demanding she fainted for a few seconds.

With her shaky fingers, she parted the hair from her face and looked up at him with rheumy eyes as he pounded away at her. "Oh my God, come for heaven's sake!"

He did in a hard thrust to the hilt, exploding inside her. The effort depleted him like a blasted dam. He cupped her face and kissed her nose, mouth and cheeks. Even with the black eye, she was as pretty as he recalled her.

"It's almost sundown," she said, seated cross-legged beside him as he brushed away her hair.

Still not fully awake, he raised himself up on his elbows and looked around the room. The shadows were long and the light, a fiery red; it was sign enough that he'd better get ready to meet Holden and Chief. It would take several hour's riding to reach Campo and then some time for the spies to find the outlaws' positions.

He dressed, pulled on a boot and she bent over and stole a kiss. Then she wrapped her head in a scarf and he had to admit in the old clothing and under the head wrap, she did look like an old woman. He hoped it worked and wiggled his toes in an effort to pull on the second boot. *Maldito, your days are numbered*, Slocum said to himself.

23

The moonlit ride to Campo proved uneventful. They parted with Donna and the Apache, who was wearing his new white unblocked felt hat, and went ahead on foot. They went around the village to a deserted old jacal in a canyon with an empty corral for the horses. They left them saddled. Christo, the guitar man, strummed his instrument while Holden and Slocum napped under the rustling cottonwoods in the rising south wind.

"What will you do after we get him and his gang?" Holden asked when Slocum sat up and yawned.

"Just keep moving on like a Kansas tumbleweed."

"I could use a good man like you at the mine on security."

Slocum shook his head. "There's a murder warrant out for me up at Fort Scott."

"You'd be surprised what I can get squashed."

"Not this one."

"Who'd find you?"

"Couple of brothers out of there. A rich man keeps them on the road looking for me."

"A new identity. Why, they'd never be the wiser."

No, I've even had funerals. It don't work."

"They that smart?"

"No, I'd call them too plain dogged."

157

"Ever consider cutting them down?"

Slocum shook his head. "He'd only hire someone smarter than them."

"Guess you know your business. But if you ever need a favor, call on me."

"I will."

It was past noon and they were chewing on their lunch of dry jerky when Chief arrived under his new felt hat, riding a burro. He slipped off the animal and nodded at them.

"What did you learn?" Holden asked, striding over.

The old man rubbed his loincloth and made a pained face. "Damn burro give me sore balls."

Chuckling at the Apache's displeasure, Slocum joined them.

"Maldito is in hotel—upstairs. Cortez is in a cantina."

"Are any of the others there, Reyas or Montoya?" Slocum asked.

"Maybe five more are in the village. They are using the cantina as headquarters and trying to recruit more men."

"Getting any takers?" Holden asked.

Chief shook his head. "Only boys are applying. He wants tough hombres."

Slocum gnawed off more of his jerky stick and looked at the pale foothills studded with dusty junipers. "He's really depleted his forces since Fronteras."

"Or are there some more around?" Holden asked.

"Good question. I say we take out the men he has one by one."

Holden agreed. "Hey, Christo, how many men has he got?"

The man put down his guitar and brushed off the seat of his pants when he got up and came over. "He had maybe a half dozen in Campo."

Chief nodded. "I think that is all he has."

"Did you see Donna?" Slocum asked the Apache.

"She is fine."

"Come dark, we start taking out his men," Holden said. "You want to help?" he asked Christo.

The man shrugged. "I am no pistolero."

"Don't have to be. We could use a prisoner guard."

"I have no gun."

"No problem. We can get you one," Holden said, sharing a look of approval with Slocum.

"Better get rested while we can," Slocum said. "We'll have a busy one tonight."

In late afternoon, the "old woman" found their camp and came in with her head wrapped in the scarf. Slocum saw her coming and sat up.

"Well, is he there?" he asked.

She squatted down beside him and nodded, undoing her scarf. "He's there all right. In a whorehouse, pretty drunk. His man Cortez is in a saloon hiring men."

"How many?"

"A few. He wants experienced pistoleros. There are only a handful in the village."

"Any of the others in town?"

"They have a camp where they keep the horses near the mission."

"How many are there?"

"Three or four. I could not be sure that some were not in the village."

"She's found their camp," Slocum said as the others joined him. "It's near the mission. Four or so. They're guarding things and the horses?"

She nodded.

"Take it first?" Holden asked, rubbing his beard stubble with his palm.

"I think so. But we need to remember the men he has left killed the Apaches."

"What were their names again?" Holden asked.

"Reyas and Montoya were the two that Chief and I know."

"You're right. This Cortez will be tough, too; he got away the last time."

Slocum thanked Donna and she smiled. No doubt in his mind that the ones that were left were the toughest ones they'd faced in this entire effort. He rose with a yawn and shook out his blanket, looking at a bleeding sunset in the far west. It would be a while before he slept again. Things would be difficult and dangerous in the night ahead.

Holden broke into his thoughts. "We go in on foot or horse-back?"

"On foot, I'd say. Slower, but we can be more cautious on foot. What do you say Chief?"

"Horses will be safe here."

"Go to the mission first?" Holden asked.

"We can start there and work out the rest," Slocum said.

"It's a good walk. Donna, you don't have to go."

Her dark eyes drew tight. "I wouldn't miss this for anything."

"It could be dangerous."

"Life is dangerous." She rose and smiled at him. "A woman's charm can distract even the toughest ones."

So they left camp and moved down a sandy arroyo out of sight. In the twilight they emerged in the vineyards of the mission. Donna led the way up the rows. Christo with the guitar on his back came last.

Slocum could see the bandits' horses and mules were tied on a picket line. Beyond that was a fire and some women were cooking, The smell of their smoke and food made Slocum's stomach complain. Everyone bellied down in the grapes and studied the movements in the camp.

One bandit walked around by the horses, and obviously, from the rifle in his arms, he was the guard.

Chief crawled over beside Slocum.

"I can get him." The Apache tossed his head in the direction of the picket line.

Slocum agreed. "Quiet."

On his hands and knees, Chief shared a nod with Holden and left them.

Where were the others? Slocum lay on the warm ground and wondered. Had they all gone to town? No, the women would not be cooking unless they expected to feed someone.

"Time to eat!" a woman shouted.

Slocum and Holden shared a smile when a man came out of a tent and stretched. Two more soon joined them. Their chatter soon filled the growing night. It was enough to hide the thump of a body hitting the ground over by the animals.

Holden nodded in approval. "When they sit down and begin eating?"

Slocum agreed and reached back for his Colt. Both men started crawling down the row. They would be out of sight most of the way. Everyone was busy eating or fixing their plates. Slocum could only see the tops of their heads in the fire's light when he lifted up.

"Paco!" a woman called toward the horses. "Supper is ready. Where is he? I can't believe he loves those horses that much to miss a meal."

The guard—she was trying to call in the horse guard. Slocum nodded to Holden. Time to move out. They both rose with their six-guns in their hands and charged the camp.

"Hands high or die," Holden shouted.

Women screamed. A man across the fire threw aside his food tray and went for his gun. Slocum knew the glare would blind him and drew aim on his chest. The Colt thundered in his right hand and the man pitched backwards. The outlaw's revolver exploded in the air. Another began to run, Holden cut him down and the third threw his hands high.

Donna began to disarm the women, taking their knifes and brusquely searching them for any weapons and forcing them to sit down. After she completed her individual searches, she ordered them to take a place on the ground.

Chief dragged in the one who had ran off. The bandit, wounded in the shoulder, was moaning out loud.

On the other side of the fire, Slocum found his man on his back. His blank eyes stared up at the stars, which were beginning to prick the darkening sky. He wondered about the gunshots warning those in the village.

"What about the horse guard?" Holden asked, as he tied up the wounded bandit.

Chief shook his head as if he would be of no concern. "He has gone to the other world."

"You see the two you're looking for?" Holden asked.

Chief glanced at Slocum, than shook his head. "Not here."

"We'd better get on to the village. They may already be on the move with all this shooting," Holden said.

"Let's get Cortez if we can," Slocum said. "I'll take him on. You and Chief surround the whorehouse and don't let Maldito out."

"Right. Christo, here take this gun and guard them. Shoot first and ask questions later."

"I am going, too," Donna said, carrying a rifle and they all began to run for the village.

They reached the edge of the jacals and many were dark.

Spread out, the four of them began to walk toward the center, taking care to observe everything.

Holden swiveled with his six-gun ready and Slocum quickly moved to cover him. Nothing but a cur dog. Some women seeing them in the starlight ran quickly aside and hugged each other in panic.

"Hush!" Donna hissed at them. They became silent except for the soft moans for their life.

Chief pointed to the left to indicate where the cantina was located. Slocum held up his hand to signal he saw it. Then he started to move in the direction of the building with the light in the open back door.

"I am coming, too," Donna said, holding up her skirt and joining him.

"He may have fled already," Slocum said under his breath.

Slocum searched around the building. As they drew closer, he noticed someone coming out the back door. He held out his hand for Donna to stop. Holding their breath, the two watched as a man fished his tool out and began to piss.

The man leaned back and arched a big stream. Donna softly chuckled at his action.

Someone with a gun in hand came to the back door and asked the man, "See anything?"

"No," the man slurred. "Just me and my big dick are out here."

"You hear shots?" the other one demanded.

Slocum traded Donna the pistol for the rifle and tried to take aim. The gunman was inside the doorway and only occasionally could he glimpse him. He needed a better target. What would get him outside?

"Scream as loud as you can," he told Donna and with the rifle to his shoulder took aim at the lighted doorway.

Her shrill scream filled the night. The figure with the gun in hand filled the doorway trying to see who'd made the outcry. Slocum squeezed off the trigger and the bullet slammed the bandit back inside. The revolver in his hand must have been cocked for it fired and the drunk began screaming, "I'm hit! I'm shot!"

"I hope that guy didn't shoot him in the dick," Donna said as they hurried across the lot.

"Big as it was it might have made a target." Slocum laughed.

"Big as he thought it was you mean," she said and they both stopped at sight of another man in the doorway.

"Don't shoot! Don't shoot!" the man cried. "I think he is dead."

"Get outside and get your hands in the air," Slocum ordered.

"I am. I am."

Slocum stopped about ten feet away. "Who was shot?"

"Senor Cortez."

"Good," Slocum said and scowled at the drunk crying and blubbering seated on the ground. "Any more of them inside?"

The man in the apron shook his head.

"He's only scratched," Donna said in disgust, standing up after checking on the drunk.

"Where did the others go?" Slocum demanded from the bartender.

"They rode away when they heard the shots."

"How many?"

"Two."

"We better go help Holden and Chief," Slocum said to her. Why did he feel those two were the killers that fled. Montoya and Reyas, still the elusive pair.

She agreed and they hurried off around the piles of broken glass bottles and trash. Behind the hotel, they joined Chief.

"Holden, him go inside."

Slocum nodded he'd heard him. "Cortez is dead."

"Good, he is where he belongs."

"Any sign of Maldito?" Slocum studied the second-story windows for any sign or movement. He could see the lights in the rooms came from small candles.

"Holden say stay here in case he comes out," Chief said.

"Yeah, someone needs to. I'd better go see if I can back him. Stay here with Chief," he said to Donna.

Gunshots began to break out inside the upstairs. Slocum began to run for the side stairs. Five, six shots. He hit the steps two at a time. Then he heard something crash out front. Out of breath, he stood in the doorway at the end of the hallway. He could see that Holden was down, waving toward the front of the building.

"He jumped out the damn window."

"How're you?'

"Don't worry about me. The bastard's getting away."

Slocum turned and piled down the stairs. He ran to the front of the building and saw where something had made a big hole in the palm frond roof of the porch. No sign of the outlaw from the corner of the building. The street was empty in the starlight. Then he heard the two-note whistle of a desert quail. Chief must be across the street. His gun hand so close to his face, he could smell the black powder and oil on the .44. He studied the night for any sign.

"Is Holden hurt?" she whispered from behind him.

"Yes, go and see about him." He gave a head toss to the stairs.

"Here." She handed him the rifle.

"Loaded?" He put the Colt away.

"Yes."

"Thanks, I may need it."

She left, her soft soles rushing up the steps.

On the porch across the street in the gloomy night were two wooden barrels and some packing crates. Maldito could be hiding behind them. Looking through the rifle's iron sights, he wondered where the Apache was. Maybe he would whistle again, so Slocum could take a shot and not hit him.

Then he heard something crash and the orange blaze of a six-gun filled Slocum's vision. In a reflex, he dodged back as dirt from the bullets flew off the side of the adobe building and blinded him for a second. He came right back firing the rifle hard pressed in his shoulder. Levering cartridges in as fast as he could. Despite his shooting, he could see the man dragging a leg he obviously must have been broken in the fall. The rifle clicked on empty. Slocum reached for the Colt but by then Maldito had managed to drag his bad leg out of sight around corner of the building.

"You want me, you bastards can come get me." His maniacal laughter filled the night.

Slocum saw the silhouette of Chief on the roof. He whistled and waved him toward the side he hoped that the outlaw was hiding on. A bob of the unblocked hat and his man moved in that direction.

"Maldito," Slocum shouted. "I'm coming for you. Get ready to die."

"Who the hell do you work for?"

"No one."

"That's bullshit. You were after my pack train. You were with the *federales* when they attacked my place." Then the laughter. "But now it's you and me. I got your partner up there. He won't live. I'll get you."

"Why don't you come out here? You and me. We'll have it out. May the best man win."

"You first."

"All right. Come on out." Slocum made enough steps to be clear of the porch.

Some long minutes went by. Then Slocum heard a grunt and some more noise from around the corner. Maldito appeared, hatless and dragging his leg.

"Your name Slo-cum?"

"They call me that."

"I had a good thing till you came down here. I had money, plenty of tough guys, a fort, a place in the Madres—" He came a few feet closer to the edge of the porch. "You ruined all that—"

"You got too greedy. You could have run mescal over the border for years and never got caught."

Maldito laughed, the same haunting laughter. "Oh, amigo, you don't know how expensive it is to live in Mexico. Smuggling alone won't pay for it."

"That's a shame. Who killed my Apaches?"

"Apaches?"

"Yes, they killed two Apaches."

"What they hell were they worth? Like pussy, cut her throat after you fuck her."

Slocum closed his eyes to the barrage of gunfire pouring down on the bandit from the upstairs over him and the far roof. Maldito spun around as slug after lead slug struck his torso. Then the guns fell silent. One more shot came from the gun hand of Donna in the upstairs window, then her pistol clicked on empty. That last one was for Mary, Slocum thought.

Slocum's ears still ringing, he shouted to the blank-eyed Donna above him. "How's Holden?"

"He'll live."

"Good."

"Chief, you all right?"

"Doing better. Much better."

24

Slocum reined up his horse and removed his dust-floured felt hat for the white woman. "Ma'am, good morning."

"Good morning to you, brother."

"I'm looking for a man named Reyas. They say he lives near here."

"You have mules to sell?" She looked distrustfully at the Apache on his paint.

"Yes, ma'am. He doesn't have all he needs yet, does he?" He went along with her, not knowing where it would lead. More than anything he wanted to know where Marco Reyas lived. This polygamous Mormon was a stern-looking woman who for his part would be equally bitchy on her back in bed.

"Why, no. He needs several. I guess bandits stole his last train. Why he wants to go back is beyond me."

"Bandits got his pack train?"

"That's what he said when he came back."

Slocum motioned southward. "His place close to this road?"

"It's on the rise above the last cotton field. The jacal up there."

"Thanks, ma'am." He reset his hat and nodded, reining the horse around to leave.

"I don't believe you!" she shouted after him. "You have no mules to sell him!"

"I would if I had some," Slocum said under his breath and the Apache grinned as they rode away.

"Me, too."

"I can tell by the look in your eyes—you two're killers. Vengeance is mine saith the Lord. You'll roast in hell and damnation. Don't you know that?"

Slocum nodded. She'd be worse in bed than he'd ever imagined. Why had God made such lovely vessels and in the midst put battle-axes like her? No telling, but it made him grateful for the good ones.

The fields of corn, vegetables, cotton and alfalfa spread over the river bottom and the desert reared its bald head in the long rise above it. A lone jacal sat on the top of the ridge and in the distance, Slocum saw a woman rush inside at the sight of them.

"He's fixing to ride off," Slocum said and stood up in the stirrups to lope his dun. Chief beside him, agreed, and they set out in a run for the far side of the farmland. Already a small streak of dust cut the azure sky. The one they wanted had fled.

No matter, the pregnant girl at the jacal when questioned denied his name was Reyas. Slocum was bone-tired and disgusted. Chief was only getting his second wind. He pointed southward. "How far can he go?"

"Vera Cruz. South America."

"He will run his horse in the ground in one day."

"Then he will buy another."

Chief looked unimpressed. "You can go back and stay with that Mormon woman until I find him."

"No, I'd rather ride with you than have to listen to her."

Chief chuckled. "Me, too."

They went on at a trot across the sea of knee-high greasewood. There was a faint trace of dust in the sky. Holden was missing all this fun, Slocum decided. They'd left him with his left arm all bandaged up from the bullet wound and Donna to look after him.

They watered their horses at a well, pulling up bucket after bucket to fill the rock trough. Reyas had left in such a hurry, he'd not destroyed the rope and pail. An act that Slocum would have expected of a fleeing felon. Perhaps Chief was right, they would ride him down by persistence. He hoped so.

Darkness came and Chief wanted to continue. Slocum offered no resistance to the idea. But he felt it strange that the Apache who hated the night would want to go on.

"I thought Apaches hated nighttime?" he asked riding beside him.

"Apaches do. But I been living as a white man for days now. It makes no difference to them about day or night."

"You're becoming a white man in your old age?"

A warm smile came to his dark lips and his hat bobbed in the twilight. "Not all bad idea."

Slocum chuckled. Yes, Holden was missing all this.

They called the village Arido. Dust-coated date palms stuck up over the walls. The gates had long before been taken down. When they rode under the archway, Slocum could see the well in the center of the square. In the peach light of early morning, they saw an obviously spent horse blowing in the dust. His breath sent up clouds of dirt at the hitch rack.

Slocum touched his hip and felt for the Colt, which had been cleaned and reloaded. "That's his horse?"

"Looks like it," Chief said and slipped off his paint horse, surveying the whole place.

"I'd say so, too." Slocum swung down, using the dun for a shield. "Probably in that cantina."

Chief nodded. "I knew we'd run him down."

"I'll go inside and see if he's there," Slocum said, stepping down and handing him the reins.

"Be careful. Trapped wolves are twice as mean as those on the run."

Slocum agreed, scratched the back of his neck below the hair line, then he set out for the dark doorway. He crossed the shadowy porch and could see over the batwing doors that a light was on inside. Beyond them, death lurked. His fist closed on the red wood grips, he cocked the .44 coming up with it.

With his left hand he pushed in the split doors. Hoping his eyes were adjusted enough to the darkness to see, he stepped though them.

"Damn you!" someone swore.

The Colt bucked in Slocum's hand. The percussion put out the lights. Slocum dodged to the side as Reyas's pistol spat orange flames from the muzzle. Acrid gun smoke boiled up in the room and Slocum aimed at the source. Ears ringing, he fired three shots and heard the crash of a body falling over chairs.

"Don't shoot! Don't shoot!" someone cried.

Slocum first saw his apron. Hands high, the bartender came through the bitter smoke.

"Get out of here." More concerned how hard the bandit was hit than the man, Slocum held the Colt ready.

He eased himself across the room until he was behind the bar. Listening to Reyas's hard breathing and cursing under his breath, Slocum set a lamp on the back bar and lit it. The flare showed up and two shots shattered the mirror beside it. It also put out the light again. Slocum, on his knees, knew the man's gun was probably empty. Five shots spent. He crawled to the end of the bar and tried to make out where Reyas was at.

The sound of someone dropping cartridges put him into action. He rounded the end of the bar. "Hands up or die."

"Damn you!" Reyas swore.

Slocum could make out the figure on his side. The outlaw raised his pistol—too late. The .44 slug took him in the forehead and slammed him on the floor. Satisfied and choked upon the gun smoke, Slocum staggered for the door. Outside, he used a porch pole for support.

"Him dead?" Chief asked still sitting on his horse.

Slocum nodded.

"One more left."

"Yeah, one more. Montoya. But first I need a drink."

"He is dead?" the bartender asked indicating the cantina.

"Yeah, go in and get us a bottle of whiskey. Me and Chief got some thinking to do."

"How 'bout mescal?"

Slocum waved him on. "Anything will be fine, right, Chief?"

"Be plenty good." He dropped off his horse. Looking around he wrinkled his wide nose as if he didn't approve. "This place is about as good as San Carlos."

They both laughed.

25

Slocum sat his spent dun horse. He'd been in the saddle more hours than he wanted to think about. Chief conversed in Spanish with a woodcutter who drove some burros loaded with sticks. At last he reined the paint horse over to where Slocum and the dun were in the center of the road.

"Montoya lives in the village ahead."

"He say he was at home?" Slocum couldn't see any village for the heat waves distorted even the distant saw-edged mountains.

Chief shook his head. "He did not know."

"I'd sure like to find him and have this over."

"They call the place Hondo."

"Hondo, Hondo, here we come."

Chief looked back at the man and nodded. "He was once an Apache. I thought I knew him."

"Looked Mexican to me."

"He was captured very young and made into a warrior. Later he choose to be with his own kind."

"He know you?"

"He said he did."

"He also said when I asked him about raids that there was going to be a wedding at your amigo's hacienda."

"Mary and Richardo?"

"Yes."

"Many plan to attend the festivities so there will not be many in the village."

"We'll get a drink in the cantina and learn all we can from there."

"Sounds good."

The small village looked empty when they drew up at the adobe building marked CANTINA in faded black letters. With an eye out for any sign of trouble, the two sauntered inside the shadowy interior.

"Good afternoon, gentlemen." The bartender flashed his white teeth at them.

"Bottle of some kind of cactus juice. Best you have," Slocum said seeing the place was empty.

"Whole town's empty?" Slocum said, taking the two glasses and the bottle from the bar.

"Ah, they have gone for the big wedding."

"You seen Montoya the last few days?"

The man's smile vanished and he looked very somber. "I know no Montoya."

"You know him. Spit it out, has he been in here lately?"

"No, senor."

With a sigh of exasperation, Slocum put the bottle and glasses back on the bar. "I don't think you savvy real good. I asked if he had been in here."

"Sometimes he doesn't come in here for days, weeks or even months, senor."

"He been in here recently?"

"Not today."

"Yesterday?"

"*Si.*"

"What time?"

"Sundown."

"Good, maybe he'll come back at sundown today."

The barkeep gave him a solemn nod.

Slocum picked up the two glasses and the bottle in his other hand. He looked hard at the man. "Don't tell him anything. We'll tell him we're here. Savvy?"

"Oh, *si*, senor."

With a grim nod at the man, he paused a second longer. "Don't try nothing. It could be fatal." Then he headed for the back table and the unblocked felt hat.

Time ticked away slow-like. The bartender ordered them food cooked by an old woman and delivered on wooden trays.

The smell of the roasted meat and fried peppers filled Slocum's nose as he wrapped some in a tortilla. Chief nodded his approval, as he did the same thing. The old woman's cooking proved to be delicious and they savored every bite.

In late afternoon, the bartender lighted candles on a wagon wheel and pulled it back up. No one came in as the day dragged on. Then there was the sound of several horses pulling up outside and five men under Chihuahua sombreros charged in and rushed to the bar. One man acted in charge, giving orders to the bartender and throwing down money. Then, as if they'd been gagged the men grew quiet. One of them used his thumb to indicate the pair in back.

The man with the mustache, who appeared to be in charge, turned and his narrow eyes glared at Slocum and Chief.

"Who the hell are you?" An ugly scar etched his cheek like a purple arroyo.

Slocum rose and nodded considering them as the others turned as if on cue. "Slocum's my name. This is Black Wolf, I call him Chief."

"You two got business here."

Slocum nodded.

"What kind of business?" The man made five steps forward. The mistake put him in any line of fire from his own men.

"To arrest you, Scar." Slocum's Colt .44 belched flames and death.

Guns rattled and in the deafening explosions, some rushed for the door and fled. Lights went out and it was over. The barkeep, with a shaky match, lighted a lamp.

Scar laid on his back. Another of his men held his bloody arm, seated on his butt on the floor while a third one was sprawled facedown next to him. Two of the bandits had gotten away.

"Go get an ax and a gunnysack," Slocum said.

The bartender frowned. "What for?"

"A wedding present for a guy I know."

Montoya never showed that evening. Perhaps warned by the gunfight, he wasn't at the jacal they said was his either. So after some sleep they rode for Richardo's hacienda.

"No sense in us missing the party," Slocum said.

"Be big party," Chief said as they rode in a long walk.

Richardo's man took the gunnysack at the gate. "It is Scar's head?"

"You'll see," Slocum said as a boy from the stables rushed over to take their horses.

"Oh, the patron will be excited," the man said, holding the sack out so it did not touch his pants.

"Good," Slocum said, then turned to the stable boy, "Rub them down and let them cool before you feed them."

Music was coming from the center of the compound. Whole beeves and sheep carcasses were cooking on spits and women rushed about getting things ready.

"Slocum! Slocum!" Richardo called out. "And you brought his head! Oh, I am so grateful! Maybe we can live here in peace again."

He wanted to tell his excited friend there was no end to the Scars in this world: one was dead, but another would rise phoenix-like from the ashes and replace him by the next sunup. But he didn't want to spoil Richardo's big event.

"Mary was so worried you'd miss our wedding," Richardo said.

"We need to clean up some—"

"No problem, come with me."

"You coming, Chief?"

The old man smiled and nodded. "More being a white man stuff, huh?"

"Like that," Slocum agreed and they both laughed.

Hours later, Slocum had bathed, shaved and wore fresh clothing provided by his host. Fiesta music carried across the hacienda's spacious gardens and the noisy party folks were having a fine time.

"I owe you so much," Mary said, dressed in a fine light-blue gown. Her hair was piled on her head then tumbled down in ringlets. A far cry from the dusty-faced defiant woman he had stopped on Mule Shoe Pass for following him.

"No, we are even. Chief has been such a great help, I'd never have done it without him. You brought him to me."

"There is still one of them left?"

"A bandit called Montoya. But we will find him."

"I thought maybe you would quit. Maldito is dead and the rest." She looked off in the night at the Chinese lights and chewed on her lower lip.

"I think Chief wants him, too. I know Duke Holden does."

"You mentioned he was wounded?"

"He's in good hands," he said thinking about Donna and her supple body.

"Be careful, Slocum." She acted ready to leave him. "I have many things to still see about."

"I hope you and my amigo are very happy, Mary."

She paused, skirt in her hands and nodded. "Oh, we will be. But I shall never forget you either."

The crack in her voice told him she was about to cry and she hurried off. He turned to look at the couples dancing and listened to the trumpet. Richardo was a lucky man—not many women would do all she did to get her first husband's killer. Slocum wondered about the night she almost slept with him. Guess he'd always wonder how that would have been.

26

Five days later, he and Chief were drinking *cerveza* in a cantina in the village of Arido. A man by the name of Jorge was supposed to meet them there. But that had been two days before and still there was no sign of the man they met at the wedding. Jorge bragged he could locate this Montoya, who was also known as Frugario Soldez. Jorge was supposed to meet them in this village and for forty pesos deliver Montoya, dead or alive. Slocum had little doubt Holden would reimburse him the money, so he and the Apache drifted over to Arido and waited and waited.

It was midafternoon, and most of the town was taking a siesta from the heat. Soon a man stuck his head in the saloon's open doorway and shouted to the bartender. "Come outside and tell me who this hombre is?"

"What did you find?" the man asked, putting down the glass he polished and ducking under the bar.

Slocum nodded to Chief, rose, stretched and started for the door to see for himself.

The man cut the body loose from the mule and the corpse fell on the ground on its back. A familiar, dusty, bloated, fly-covered face stared at the too-bright azure sky with wide open eyes.

"Who knows this man?" the bartender asked, looking over the curious that death attracts. "You know him?" he asked Slocum.

Slocum shook his head. "Where did you find him?" He asked the man dressed in white clothing who had brought the body.

"At Arrow Springs."

"I guess someone didn't like him. Shot several times at close range. Powder burns on his shirt."

The man nodded.

"Take his body to the magistrate," the bartender said, waving some men in to carry it. "This is a job for the *rurales* to investigate."

"Will they?" Slocum asked.

The bartender turned and looked him in the eye. "No, but they are supposed to."

Inside, Slocum took his chair and pushed the felt hat back. In a soft voice, he began, "Our man Jorge is dead. They found his body at Arrow Springs. Someone shot him four or five times in the chest at close range."

Chief nodded. "Then the man is close to here or he was."

"My thoughts exactly. He's maybe watching us."

"He knows you from that night we had them."

"He also knows I'm gringo and in this land there are not many others."

"What should we do?"

"Find us a new source of information."

Chief nodded and chuckled. "We need that for sure."

Slocum turned when a woman came in the doorway and her beauty immediately struck him. This was no ordinary housewife coming for a bucket of *cerveza* or a *puta* looking for someone to buy her time in a hammock. Her high cheekbones and flawless complexion topped a body ripe as a Georgia peach. She walked toward him like a willow tree swept in a soft breeze.

"Senor?"

He rose and removed his hat. "Ma'am."

"I am Senora Theresa Ramono Martinez."

"They call me Slocum."

"I know your name. My casa is only a short distance from here. May we adjourn to my place? I need to talk with you."

He squeezed his chin and considered her ripe body under the expensive dress. "That would suit me fine." From his pocket he drew out a ten-peso gold piece. "Pay the bar bill, Chief, when you get through. See you at the horses later."

The Apache nodded and a small smile cracked his deep, wrinkled, copper-colored lips. "I can do that."

Slocum followed the woman out the door. Somehow he felt like a sheep going to slaughter. Nothing amiss as they went up the street with Theresa carrying her long dress in her hands.

"You have been here several days they say." She glanced up at him for an answer.

"A few."

"You have business in Arido?"

"I had hoped to do some but the man I hoped to do it with has taken leave."

"Do I know his name?" She stopped at some outside stairs that led up the side of the building to the upstairs.

"Jorge Artega."

"Hmm, never heard of him. This way to my casa," she said and started up the stairs.

With a last search of the street, he saw nothing out of place and then started after her.

The apartment was spacious, nice enough, but somehow not the place where he expected she resided. She opened the French door to the porch.

"That should let some more air in," she said and smiled coming across the tile floor, shedding the scarf and shaking loose her long black hair. "Put your hat on the table."

He hooked it on the chair back and nodded when she beckoned him to join her on the sofa.

"You wonder why I have asked you up here?"

"I could wonder," he said, looking into the pools of brown that stirred him up.

"I am a widow."

He nodded.

"I need to hire someone to help me get my mine back—the one my husband had before he died. It's been taken over by bandits."

"You probably need an army, not me."

She dropped her gaze to her hands in lap. "I need someone to gather that army."

"Do I look like I could raise an army in Mexico?"

Her long hand reached out and ran down his cheek. It felt like a butterfly's wings beating a flower's petals and at last came to rest on his leg. "You are my last chance." Her smoky, pleading voice trailed off.

"Maybe we should get to know each other better," he said, moving closer and raising her chin with the side of his hand.

She closed her long, dark lashes and pursed her lips. Their mouths became cemented and he wrestled her into his arms. She shoved her firm breasts into him and hot air raged out of his nostrils.

When at last they came free for air, her palms pressed on his chest. "Give me a few moments?"

"Fine, but don't run off," he said then rose, taking her hand and helping her up.

"Oh, I would never do that," she said and disappeared into the next room.

He unbuckled his gun belt, looked at the open door and quickly removed the Colt and emptied the cartridges from the cylinder. The gun replaced in the holster hung under his hat and the loose shells were in his pocket. He glanced at the doorway.

"Come in here," she coaxed.

"Coming," he said and crossed the living space to the doorway pausing to look at the great feather bed under a canopy. Beside it, dressed in a filmy silk nightgown, stood Theresa.

"Ah, you have no gun," she said and slid her arms around him.

"I didn't come to do that kind of shooting."

She threw her head back and laughed openly. "No, not that kind."

Her nimble fingers unbuttoned his shirt and pulled it off over his head. He toed off his boots, then began to unbutton his pants. With a pause, he looked at her for approval. When she nodded, he continued and stripped them off with his socks.

In the next instant she slipped against him and their mouths met. He pushed the filmy gown off her shoulders. Her warm flesh pressed against his. He knew his rising erection was poking her.

He reached under her legs and tossed her lightly onto the bed, then he followed. An ache in his butt hungered to thrust his swollen dick in her to the hilt. She scooted to be underneath him and raised her parted knees. He found the track and drove the nail home. Pounding her as hard as he could, she cried out for more.

The world began to spin and his efforts caused the raging breath to hurt his lungs. More and more and more. They were on fire and no end in sight for their lust. Sweat lubricated their bellies and she cried out, "Oh, dear God—"

He drove his swollen sword as deep as he could go. Grasping both sides of her butt in his iron grip to force his way, he fired his cannon. The explosion went off in his head and inside of her. She fainted.

He lay there in a deep sleep. It was past sundown when he awoke. In the candlelight, he stared into the muzzle of his own revolver, which Theresa held in both hands. The gown was buttoned to the throat and she was on her knees, pointing the Colt at him.

"You know who I am?" She cocked back the hammer.

"Arana Cortez."

She blinked her eyelids at him in shock and shoved the gun more threateningly at him. "How do you know that?"

"Made sense. Why else would a beautiful woman like you come looking for some drifter like me?"

"You killed my husband and my brother."

"And you're going to kill me."

Her eyes glinted with her rage.

"Well, you better get on with it. I kinda wanted to have another toss in the hay with you. Fact is if you miss shooting me, I might just do that to you again."

"No, you won't—" She drew her head up.

"I may just do that."

She shut down her lashes to glare at him. "You—you aren't even afraid of dying?"

"Why don't we make love one more time?"

"No. I'm going to kill you."

"Ever kill anyone before?"

"No—"

"Good." He brushed the gun barrel aside.

"You killed—"

"No, they killed some innocent men in their greed. I came to arrest them."

"I'm going to kill you!" she screamed and forced the gun back in his face.

He sat and grinned. "Go ahead. It's harder than you thought it would be, right?"

"No . . . no . . . I'm going to . . . kill . . . you."

With his left hand he pushed the pistol away, with his right hand pulled her toward him. Her words that she was going to kill him were soon smothered by his lips on hers.

27

Under an azure sky and a hot sun bearing down on them, they rode into the junipers and live oaks. A cooling breeze struck Slocum's face when he turned the blue roan up the canyon. The sullen-faced prisoner Montoya came next on a bay, then Chief riding a black piebald. Under a blue parasol, riding sidesaddle on a bloodred chestnut came Senora Theresa Ramono Martinez.

"Be cooler up on top of this pass," Slocum said over his shoulder.

"I can hardly wait," she said.

Sundown, they were at the courthouse in Bisbee. News of their arrival must have preceded them for Duke Holden was at the jail with Madden when they arrived.

"I see you and the old man got him," Holden said with a grin.

Slocum nodded. "The last one." He shoved Montoya toward the man.

Holden must have noticed Theresa standing behind them. He jerked off his hat and stepped towards her. "We've never met ma'am."

"No, but I have heard much about you, Senor Holden."

"You guys can handle this," Holden said. "Call me Duke, please."

Her hand on his arm, they were soon gone out the office door. Madden scratched his thinning hair. "He ran off with your girl?"

181

Slocum shook his head. "No, I owed him a favor."

"Wished you owed me one like that."

"Holden owes Chief and me some money and he got away."

"You leaving already?"

Slocum nodded. He wasn't going to explain to the man that the big horse hitched in the street below belonged to a Kansas deputy sheriff he knew.

"How much?"

"A hundred dollar apiece."

"I can get my hands on that much—but—"

"What?"

"I figured we'd have a big meal together, celebrate and you'd tell me all about how it went in Mexico."

"We'd better get going."

"Well, folks in this town will always be grateful for all you've done."

The moon slipped over New Mexico and shone down on Bisbee. Slocum clapped the Apache on the arm. "Till the next time when our paths cross, amigo."

Chief's eyes even in the night looked tired. "I have enjoyed being a white man with you. I will go back to San Carlos. I think the afterlife for an Apache is better than yours."

"It sure might be," Slocum said and mounted the roan.

An hour later he looked back at the lights of Bisbee from the top of the pass. Maybe he'd go stay with Leona awhile in Fronteras—he could use some rest.

Watch for

**SLOCUM AND THE
APACHE BORDER INCIDENT**

328th novel in the exciting SLOCUM series
from Jove

Coming in June!

JAKE LOGAN
TODAY'S HOTTEST ACTION WESTERN!

Don't miss a year of

Slocum Giant

BY

Jake Logan

Slocum Giant 2003:

The Gunman and the Greenhorn

0-515-13639-5

Slocum Giant 2004:

Slocum in the Secret Service

0-515-13811-8

Slocum Giant 2005:

Slocum and the Larcenous Lady

0-515-14009-0

**Available wherever books are sold or at
penguin.com**

B900

**Explore the exciting Old West with one
of the men who made it wild!**

GIANT-SIZED ADVENTURE FROM AVENGING ANGEL LONGARM.

LONGARM AND THE UNDERCOVER MOUNTIE
0-515-14017-1

THIS ALL-NEW, GIANT-SIZED ADVENTURE IN THE POPULAR ALL-ACTION SERIES PUTS THE "WILD" BACK IN THE WILD WEST.

U.S. MARSHAL CUSTIS LONG AND ROYAL CANADIAN MOUNTIE SEARGEANT FOSTER HAVE AN EVIL TOWN TO CLEAN UP—WHERE OUTLAWS INDULGE THEIR WICKED WAYS. BUT FIRST, THEY'LL HAVE TO STAY AHEAD OF THE MEANEST VIGILANTE COMMITTEE ANYBODY EVER RAN FROM.

J. R. ROBERTS

THE GUNSMITH